FOR

GOLDEN GATE JUMPER SURVIVORS SOCIETY

"Strange circumstances abound . . . The book's many surreal elements are grounded in authentic, sometimes heartbreaking, details . . . Throughout the compelling, unexpected, and poignant stories of *Golden Gate Jumper Survivors Society*, the absurd is masked by the everyday." —**Foreword Reviews**

"Funny and deft and weird and heartbreaking. This book is super cool and one of a kind." —**Kate Durbin**

"Poignant and elegiac and full of calm desperation, Ross Wilcox's short story collection is a parable of survival—the remains of people and places, traces of presence—and the search for some kind of truth, however fallible and fleeting. Wilcox rejoices in the bizarre and absurd, but also attends to the mundanities of everyday life with deft precision. Reading *Golden Gate Jumper Survivors Society* is an unnerving experience, in which death and life, the dead and the living, converge." —**Chris Campanioni, author of *A and B and Also Nothing* and *the Internet is for real***

"From the seemingly impossible to the devastatingly real, the stories in Ross Wilcox's *Golden Gate Jumper Survivors Society* serve as touching portraits of everyday Americans. Leavened with dry humor, the collection delivers us the country-road bonfires, suburban rivalries and unattainable aspirations of the hopeful and the disillusioned, the survivors and the strugglers, the green and the seasoned—from a writer who has mastered the short story form. Wilcox's characters will continue to pester you for a smoke and ask for a ride long after the stories have ended."
—**Farooq Ahmed, author of *Kansastan***

GOLDEN GATE
JUMPER SURVIVORS
SOCIETY

stories by

Ross Wilcox

7.13 Books
Brooklyn

Printed in the United States of America

First Edition
1 2 3 4 5 6 7 8 9

The following stories originally appeared in these journals: "Golden Gate Jumper Survivors Society" in *The Carolina Quarterly*, "Broken Vessel" in *Beloit Fiction Journal*, "Year of Our Lawn" in *Columbia Journal*, "Nora's Sweatshirt" in *Nashville Review*, "Oliver Weston GBV" in *H.O.W. Journal*. "Of Small Account" in *Harpur Palate*, "Puddin' Suitcase" in *North American Review*, "Costuming" in *The Madison Review* (awarded Chris O'Malley Prize in Fiction 2017), "Symptoms" in *The Baltimore Review*, "Ransom" in *Ascent*, "Backwater" in *Midwest Review*.

Cover art by Matthew Revert
Edited by Josh Denslow

Library of Congress Cataloging-in-Publication Data

ISBN: 978-1-7333672-4-0
LCCN: 2020930236

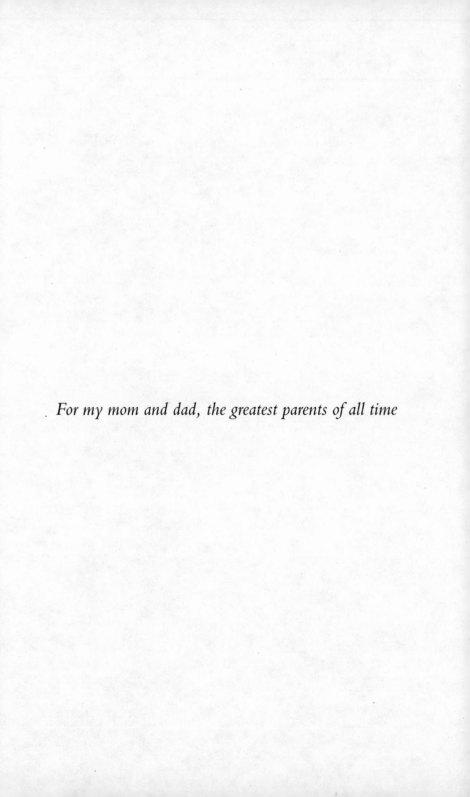

For my mom and dad, the greatest parents of all time

GOLDEN GATE JUMPER
SURVIVORS SOCIETY

THE FIRST NIGHT BONNIE showed up in the basement of the First
Unitarian Church on Franklin Street, I was still president. She
didn't at all look like your typical Jumper-off-the-street. Rather,
with her galaxy-patterned yoga pants, matching tank top, and
thick, swoopy auburn hair, she looked refreshed and healthy,
almost *happy* to have discovered us.

I was as riveted as everyone else when she told her Jumping
story, how her mind racked with regret over the life she'd never
lead in the four elongated seconds in which she fell 245 feet
through the night air before colliding with the black waters of the
Pacific Ocean.

I believed her until John Diaz, who jumped back in 1992, asked,
"Where'd you jump from?"

It was a common question. We all generally knew where
we'd jumped: what side of the bridge (east or west), what end
of the bridge (north or south), and roughly what numbered
light pole (1-128). For example, John, like most, jumped off
the east side, near light pole sixty-five at the bridge's center.
Fiona Struthers, who jumped when she was high on PCP, did
it by light pole ninety-five, a popular spot for depressed teens
who grew up in the Mission. Me, I wanted to be different. So

far, I'm the only one on record to have jumped from light pole eighty-six on the west-central side.

Prior to my Presidency, I was Bridge Duty Coordinator for seven years, longer than anyone had ever served in that position. No one knows the 4,200 feet of railing, chords, metal, and concrete of that bridge as well as I. So when Bonnie said she'd jumped from light pole forty-three, I knew she was either lying or she had misspoken. Were she to have actually jumped from light pole forty-three, which is on the northeastern side of the bridge, she'd have landed on the northern tip of Marin County, not in the Pacific Ocean.

No one else caught this discrepancy, and after she'd said it, as is our custom, the others circled around her in a group hug and welcomed her to the Golden Gate Jumper Survivors Society.

Her appearance happened to correlate with the remaining weeks of my second two-year presidential term. I'd won the first two elections unopposed and figured I was about to win a third.

But all that changed when, after only a month as a member, Bonnie stood up when I asked if there was any new business and said, "I would like to officially announce my bid for the 2015 GGJSS Presidency!"

To my horror, everyone cheered and smiled. In fact, they stood from their chairs and encircled her in hugs as they had that first night.

I thought: Hello, people. I'm right here.

I'm *right here*.

Believe me, I wanted to ask Bonnie about her sketchy Jumping story. Every time I walked past light pole forty-three while on Bridge Duty, I thought about her Jumping and landing on the patch of rocky grass along the shore rather than in the ocean. But Bonnie became so beloved so fast that I felt if I questioned her, it would just get back to everyone and look like a muckraking campaign move and only serve to alienate the seven-person electorate.

And there were other things besides the initial Jumping story that were off. For example, Bonnie's reluctance to engage in my weekly Aquatic Jumping Simulation Exercises at the Y.

Every Tuesday, for one hour, we reserved the Olympic diving board at the YMCA on Sacramento Street. We did this to satiate our individual cravings to Jump, sort of like jump methadone. Atop the diving board, we imagined climbing the railing of the lower exterior footpath and, if you were a West Side Jumper, looking out over the mounds of Hawk Hill and the Pacific, or, if you were an East Side Jumper, the city jutting out into the Bay and Oakland in the distance.

I had invented the Aquatic Jumping Simulation Exercises four years ago. They were my single greatest achievement as president. In fact, they were kind of the only thing I had achieved, and I had basically rested on the laurels of the jumping simulations for the subsequent duration of my political career.

Still, the Jumping Simulation Exercises had become our Central Bonding Activity, a thing I'd read is necessary for the unity of any organization. In the allotted sixty minutes, we'd show up and Jump as many times as we could, sometimes together and holding hands, sometimes shouting things like "Goodbye, world!" or "Nothing happens when you die!" because none of us were actually religious. We couldn't get enough of it. That's what made us Jumpers. There was no such thing as being nervous or hesitant to Jump.

But it was different with Bonnie.

She'd put on her red, one-piece bathing suit and, with a towel wrapped around her waist, stand to the side and watch us. She looked like a lifeguard and she acted like a cheerleader.

"Great Jump, Derrick!" she'd shout after Derrick Ash did his signature Cannon Ball Jump.

"Way to go, Beth!" she'd yell after Beth Fuller performed her perfected stiff-as-a-board Pencil Jump, leaving behind no splash whatsoever.

And each time someone Jumped, they'd swim to the side of

the pool and Bonnie would be there to help them out and pat them on the back. For Chris Swinton and Arnie Borland, two middle-aged, chronically single rock-collecting enthusiasts, the Aquatic Jumping Simulation Exercises became a race to Jump as often as possible so they could be touched on the back by Bonnie.

It was, I thought, shameless. A transparent baby-kissing political maneuver. What shocked me was how no one else found Bonnie's refusal to Jump suspicious. I wanted to say out loud: Is she even one of us if she won't Jump? Are you really going to elect an outsider as president?

I know, I know. *Outsider* is a harsh word.

But seriously, what kind of Jumper doesn't Jump?

And then there was Gregory Seward.

Greg was almost the most famous Jumper ever when, back in July of 1995, he was poised to be the one-thousandth suicide on the Golden Gate Bridge. He had made it a point to advertise this and all the news stations were there to film it.

Alas, like the rest of us, he hit the water at a slight angle and survived.

Greg was very well preserved at forty-five: handsome, ripply-muscled with shaggy blonde hair. In the ensuing twenty years since his Jump, he'd become a hotshot yoga instructor in the Bay Area. We'd been trying for years to get him to join the Society as our token sort-of-celebrity member, but he always refused. "I'm holding out to be the two-thousandth now," he told me with a smirk each time I, as president, diplomatically asked him to join. I'd pretty much given up on recruiting him.

At our first and only presidential debate, Bonnie hit me with the Greg Seward haymaker.

"If elected," she said, her shimmery auburn hair perfectly parted and fluffed, "I will deliver Greg Seward to this Society. That is my promise to you!"

That was basically it. The debate was over, and, for that matter, the election. They sprung from their seats, cheering like hooligans, and smothered her in hugs.

The next week I lost the election unanimously 7–0 (candidates weren't allowed to vote). And the week after that, at Bonnie's first official meeting as president, Greg Seward showed up and joined the Golden Gate Jumper Survivors Society.

You'd think it would only be polite to appoint the guy you just whooped in the election as your VP, right? But no. Frickin' Greg. Bonnie's first order of business as la presidenta was to appoint Greg Seward, who'd been a member for all of three minutes, as her VP.

I had to pinch myself for what came next.

"Now, I've been thinking some change would be good around here," Bonnie began, "which is why instead of Aquatic Jumping Simulation Exercises as our Central Bonding Activity, I thought we could try something I've designed: Yoga Jumping Simulation Practice."

She let the new idea brew in silence for a few moments. Everyone else was staring straight ahead at Bonnie. I was the only one looking side to side with a can-you-believe-this-crap? mug.

"What exactly is Yoga Jumping Simulation Practice?" asked Fiona Struthers.

Bonnie pointed at Fiona. "That's a great question, Fiona, and thank you for asking it. Yoga Jumping Simulation Practice is a new form of yoga I invented in which the yogi poses in ways that simulate jumping off a bridge."

"Isn't bridge a yoga pose?" said Chris Swinton.

"It is!" said Bonnie. "That's good, Chris."

"Wow. It seems like yoga is really well suited for Jumping Simulation because it has the bridge pose," said Arnie Borland.

Mutterings of approval trickled through the crowd. Consensus: Yoga Jumping Simulation sounded like a good idea.

"Are you people serious?" I said, in retrospect, much louder and angrier than I meant to. "Yoga Jumping Simulation? You've *got* to be kidding me."

All eyes were on me, but everyone was quiet, waiting to see how Bonnie handled my outburst.

"Do you have an objection to the yoga idea, Victor?" she asked.

"Yeah," I said. "It's ridiculous. It's not even Jumping. It's stretching."

"Have you tried it?" said Beth Fuller, coming to Bonnie's defense.

"Yeah, Vic, you shouldn't judge it before trying it," said John Diaz. "That's prejudice."

"Yeah, Vic. You're *prejudiced*," said Chris Swinton.

Bonnie crossed her arms and smirked at me. That's when I knew, or at least strongly suspected, that she was changing the Simulation program to something she liked because she was scared to Jump, because she hadn't ever Jumped, because she wasn't one of us.

I stood up and pointed at her. "She's not one of us and she never Jumped!"

For about six extremely long seconds, there was complete silence. Then someone giggled and Fiona said, "Victor, that's ridiculous."

"*Somebody's* jealous of losing the Presidency," said Chris Swinton.

"Talk about defamation of character," said Arnie Borland.

Then Greg Seward, aka Mr. Yoga of San Fran, spoke up.

"I think Yoga Jumping Simulation Practice sounds like a great idea," he said.

And that made it official. We were going to do yoga.

It got worse. That is, for me.

It got better for Bonnie.

The first day we showed up for Yoga Jumping Simulation Practice, about twenty other strangers joined us in the Y's yoga room. Bonnie and Greg Seward were at the front, right by the wall of mirrors, clad in matching tie-dye yoga pants and tank tops.

We the Jumpers laid our mats next to each other in a little

corner of the room, unsure if we were doing it right. The regular yogis looked at us like, *Who are these people with rental mats?*

Bonnie clapped her hands and said, "Okay, yogis. Let's begin in child's pose."

The regular yogis crouched on their mats, their legs tucked under their chests, their arms flat and outstretched above their heads. My fellow Jumpers looked at each other and shrugged and did their best to follow suit.

Except me.

I defiantly stared straight ahead at Bonnie and she stared back, coldly. She said, "Now slowly come up into down dog."

There was no stopping her. The Jumpers fell into the yoga practice, smiling and trying their hardest, forgetting all about the notion that this was supposed to be Yoga *Jumping* Simulation. And they only got more into it when, halfway through, Greg Seward himself took the reins and said, spiritedly, "Now let's try warrior pose, yogis. Yeah! Can you feel that burn?! *Ooooh.*"

At the beginning of the practice, Bonnie said that if at any time we didn't think we could handle it to just go into child's pose indefinitely. For the last half hour, that's what I did. But not because I couldn't handle it. Rather, because I couldn't *stand* it.

It didn't matter how quickly you could snap from standing-mountain-back-bend into bridge pose. Or how highly you arched your back. And it didn't matter how well you could do crow, tree, side angle, dolphin, pigeon, dancer, headstand, or any of the other jokey poses.

It never remotely felt like Jumping. How could it have?

Afterwards, all the regular yogis shook hands with Bonnie and Greg and thanked them for the "enlightening" practice. As we Jumpers rolled up our rental mats, Bonnie came up to us and said, "That was great, guys! Now, the first class is always free, but next time, you'll have to pay twelve dollars or you can talk to Sally at the front desk about our monthly rates. Right now, we're offering a special where the first month is only forty! That's unlimited yoga classes for only forty dollars!"

Then she pranced over to Greg and, in front of all of us, planted one on his lips.

Before I could say anything, Beth Fuller said, "Can you believe it?! Only forty dollars and we get to do as much yoga as we want!"

"That's so awesome," said Fiona Struthers.

By now I wasn't surprised that the other Jumpers agreed.

"Hold on a minute," I said. "You actually *liked* the yoga? I didn't think it felt like Jumping at all."

"Who cares? I thought it felt awesome," said Fiona.

Everyone nodded.

"I think I like it more than the Aquatic Jumping Simulation Exercises," said Arnie Borland, his eyes on Bonnie's yoga butt at the front of the room.

"Me too," said Chris Swinton.

I held up a clenched fist. "I don't think it serves our Society's needs the way the Aquatic Jumping Simulation Exercises does."

"Our needs as a Jumpers' Society are changing," said Fiona, to which the others said *Yeah*. "We want to do yoga now."

"That's bullshit," I blurted.

"God, Victor," said Beth. "Get over yourself. Just because we don't want to do your exercises anymore doesn't mean you have to be a little baby about it."

"BS," I said, being a little more PC.

The others shook their heads.

Greg approached with a big smile and said, "Come on, gang. Let's get you signed up for those monthly memberships."

They cheered while I stood there fuming. They followed Greg out the yoga room door. I pulled Bonnie aside and, after the others had disappeared down the hallway, asked, "Bonnie, why are you doing this?"

"Isn't it obvious, Victor?" she said. "I want to make a difference in these people's lives."

"But we're *Jumpers.*"

"You're yogis now," Bonnie said, pushing the door open and heading down the hallway.

"Dammit!" I yelled, my voice echoing and slightly terrifying because of how empty the room was and how it sort of symbolized the way no one listened to me anymore.

I guess I'm the kind of person who's either the star of the show or doesn't participate.

I refused to do yoga not just because it had nothing to do with Jumping, but also because it cost money. The Y had let us use the pool for free to do Aquatic Jumping Simulation Exercises because we were—or at least told them we were—a suicide prevention nonprofit. I couldn't stand the thought of Bonnie and Greg profiting off our Society. That's *so* not what the GGJSS stands for and I conveyed as much at the next weekly meeting.

I pounded my fist on the table and said, "God dammit" right in the middle of a group discussion about the virtues of eagle pose. No, it wasn't tactful, but by this point I was kind of losing it. At any rate, it got everyone's attention.

I pointed at Bonnie and Greg. "Can't you see? These two are ruining this organization. I mean, hell-o, people! This is the Golden Gate *Jumper Survivors* Society, not some yoga club."

I stood from my chair and got in Chris Swinton and Arnie Borland's faces. "You remember when it didn't cost anything to belong to GGJSS?" Then I turned to Beth Fuller and Fiona Struthers. "Now all of a sudden this redheaded robber baron comes along and we're paying monthly memberships to perform exercises that have nothing to do with Jumping. And where's that money going?" I pointed at Bonnie and Greg. "Right into their pockets, that's where!"

"Victor, I think you should sit down and be quiet," said Beth Fuller.

"Can't you just accept that we all like yoga now and move on?" asked John Diaz.

"No!!!" I screamed, literally at the top of my lungs. It was rather blood-curdling. I turned to our president. "I will not let you steal this Society from me, Bonnie."

Greg stood, poised to restrain me if necessary. The others shook their heads in pity the way people do when they witness a once great man cracking up.

"I'll start my own Jumpers' Society," I said. "Come on! Who's with me?" I beckoned wildly with my arms, though no one stood. Greg crossed his arms and chuckled.

"You think it's funny?" I said, lunging at Greg.

Chris Swinton blocked me with his rock-hard forearm. "Easy there, Vic," he said.

I retreated from the table.

"Come on!" I repeated. "Who's with me?"

No one did anything. They just glanced back and forth between Bonnie and me.

"Victor, I think you should go," Bonnie said.

"I *am* going," I said. "And I'm starting my own Jumpers' Society. And it's going to be better than this shitty one that has turned its back on its roots!"

I slammed the door shut on my way out. As I ran up the stairs to the church's main floor I yelled, "FUCK!"

Linda, the sweet, white-haired secretary of the First Unitarian Church, happened to be walking past carrying some files.

"I'm sorry," I said, almost violently.

Most presidents live a nice, relaxed, cushioned life after they leave office.

Not me. I was just angry, bitter, and jealous.

And, I realized, as Linda shook her head and kept walking, I was also a jerk.

Of course I didn't start my own Jumpers' Society. There weren't any other Jumpers. They already belonged to what I started calling the Old Society. But I couldn't help it. I kept reporting for Bridge Duty.

You see, the Golden Gate Jumper Survivors Society was basically my whole life. Before GGJSS, my life was a mess—hence the suicide attempt. Just over ten years ago, in the span of three months, my mom died in a car accident, my fiancée left me to pursue a law degree, and I accidentally locked two girls in a locker room over a weekend at Balboa Junior High, after which I was blacklisted from any custodial positions in the Bay Area.

With no mom, no fiancée, and no career, I decided to Jump.

The only thing worse than failing at life was failing at attempting to end life. That is, until I discovered the GGJSS by pure good luck. After my Jump, I was fished out of the water by a passing boat and taken to the California Pacific Medical Center on Castro Street where of all people, Beth Fuller was my nurse. She invited me to the weekly meeting at First Unitarian Church.

My first night in the Church basement I remember clearer than any memory. I could barely tell my Jumping story, so frequently did I break out into sobs. Afterwards, they all hugged me, just like they had Bonnie. I cried and cried. They didn't even hold the business portion of the meeting that night. They just sat and listened to me blubber on about Taylor, my ex-fiancée, and how I stupidly locked those seventh graders in the locker room.

I remember John Diaz grasping my hand and saying, "It's going to be okay." And I remember how old Lisa Moore, may she rest in peace, held me in her brittle arms and said, "Victor, you're one of us. Welcome home."

So no, I don't take it lightly when some outsider comes in and masquerades as a Jumper to grow her fledgling yoga business (if that's what Bonnie was in fact doing). I mean, I got on disability so that I could devote myself full-time to first Bridge Duty Coordinator and later, as you well know, president.

For me, it wasn't a choice. Even though I quit attending the weekly meetings and the Yoga Jumping Simulation Practices, I couldn't *not* report for Bridge Duty. No one was as good at it as me. I can walk the 1.7 miles of footpath in less than twenty minutes, my head swiveling around for any would-be Jumpers.

I'm the only one who can say they haven't had any successful Jumps while on Bridge Duty. I do whatever it takes. I've grabbed people's shirts and pulled them back. I've grabbed people's ponytails and yanked them back. I've shouted false things from a distance like "Watch out for the incoming terrorist missile!" to distract would-be Jumpers from Jumping until I can get there and either talk them down or pull them back. Like I said, whatever it takes.

And it was on my now unofficial Bridge Duty in the subsequent weeks after leaving the GGJSS that I heard about Bonnie's decline.

I'd run into my fellow Jumpers along the footpaths mornings and afternoons and get little updates.

"They found a lump on her left breast," Arnie Borland said, pinching the flab around his pectoral.

"But they don't know if it's malignant yet," said Fiona Struthers, her eyes suddenly red and moist. "They don't know yet. You know? They don't know."

A week or so later, Beth Fuller gave me the whole scoop. They'd done a biopsy on Bonnie at the California Pacific Medical Center where Bonnie worked. It was bad. Stage Four bad. They had to start chemo immediately.

"She knew all along she'd get it," said Beth. "She inherited it."

"Is she still holding the yoga practices? Is she still president?" I asked.

"Jesus, Victor," Beth said, shaking her head. "None of that matters anymore."

She stormed off, but only for about five steps. Then she about-faced and came back at me with fury, her face flushed red.

"You know, I came here to tell you she admitted to us that

she never Jumped. And yeah, we were pissed, but the woman has *terminal cancer*, Victor. And she's our friend. She showed us yoga."

Beth turned to leave.

"Wait," I said.

She stopped.

"Do you actually like yoga more than Jumping Simulation?"

"What is wrong with you?!" Beth screamed. Then she stormed off for real.

Which left me to wrestle with the question: What *was* wrong with me?

I never went to see Bonnie. Instead, most days, I just walked up and down the footpath of the bridge. I felt guiltier each time I talked with a fellow Jumper, although *talked* really isn't the right word.

They wanted nothing to do with me, and I practically had to force any news out of them.

"She's not doing yoga anymore," Chris Swinton told me one morning, his eyes cast towards the ocean and the rising sun. Then he glared at me and walked away.

"Greg Seward left her," John Diaz said. "That little weasel was just trying to steal clients from her at the Y."

I wanted to know just how bad the cancer had gotten. One afternoon I saw Beth Fuller. I tried to sneak up to her but she spotted me and took off at a brisk clip. I gave chase until she turned and screamed, "If you don't quit following me I'll call the police!"

I was left to stand by light pole forty-three and wonder.

Was Bonnie shriveled up, her skin gone pale ivory and sickly? Was Bonnie throwing up everything she ate? Had she lost her gorgeous auburn hair? For some reason, the thought of Bonnie's auburn hair falling out in clumps bothered me terribly and I went directly from light pole forty-three to the Y for some much-needed Aquatic Jumping Simulation Exercises.

That day, for the first time, I cut in front of children in line at the high board.

I continued walking the bridge. But I hadn't seen anyone in weeks. Just strangers. One day I stopped near light pole ninety-seven, right by the San Francisco tower, and hung my head. I didn't really know what I was doing anymore and, more importantly, why I was doing it. When I looked up, someone had climbed the railing at light pole eighty-five some fifty yards from me.

I sprinted.

As I got closer, I saw that it was a young man, maybe twenty-five years old, though it was hard to tell. The closer I got to him, the more I thought he looked like me ten years ago: long brown hair tied in a ponytail, white T-shirt, cargo shorts, Birkenstocks.

I didn't get there in time. He Jumped.

The other pedestrians leaned over the railing to peer into the ocean. But I just sat there on the concrete. I didn't have to look. Somehow, I knew he was dead.

I was at the end of my rope. I'd failed at Bridge Duty, the one thing I'd ever really done well in life. I quit doing Aquatic Jumping Simulation Exercises and instead just walked the bridge from sunup to sundown, up the West Side, and back down the East Side.

I started to think about Jumping again.

I mean, why not?

But one day, as I approached light pole forty-three, I saw her.

I recognized her immediately. From a distance, her auburn hair looked thicker and more radiant than ever. She waved at me and, as I passed light pole forty-seven, I wondered if she was faking the cancer, too.

I walked right up to her and saw, however, that the hair was a façade.

She looked terrible. She was much thinner. Her shoulders drooped and her chest hung. Her skin had paled, her eye sockets had darkened and sunk. There were pockmarks on her face. She looked ready to crumble at any moment.

"I owe you an apology," she said, her voice softer and raspy.

I felt feverishly hot, my eyes suddenly moist.

"You were right. I never Jumped."

I shook my head and covered my mouth as she removed the wig. "Don't," I said.

"No," she said, the pale dome of her head exposed and reflective in the sunlight. "I want to set the record straight. I already apologized to the others but now I want to say sorry to you for lying about Jumping."

That did it for me. "Your hair," was all I could say before I covered my face and cried. I felt worse for Bonnie than I ever had for myself, even back when I wanted to Jump.

I felt her weak fingers batting at my waist, and I saw that she was trying to hold my hand. I grabbed it and continued to cry for I don't know how long. As long as it took to stop feeling like complete shit, I guess.

When I stopped, she chuckled to herself.

"You know," she said, "after that first night, I came out here the next day and checked where light pole forty-three was and after that, I only hoped no one would remember what I'd said."

"It's okay," I said.

We were silent for a while just watching the people pass us by, letting the sun beat down on us. Then Bonnie started groaning.

She winced and said, "It fucking hurts, Victor."

I didn't know what to say, so I said, "I'm sorry."

She squeezed my hand and said, "I came here to ask you a favor. I don't want to keep going. I don't want to do any more treatments."

I realized what she wanted and said, "No, Bonnie. Please, don't."

"I want to Jump," she said.

"Don't."

"I need your help, though. I can't climb up there by myself. I'm too weak."

"I can't. I can't help you do that."

"But you got to," Bonnie said. "You got to Jump. Isn't it only fair that I get to, too?"

"Why would you ask me to do this?"

She winced again and said, "I thought you would understand. You know what it's like to want to Jump."

There wasn't anyone around.

She smirked and said, "You know, I *am* still president. You still have to do what I say."

Maybe we could do it. Make it quick.

"Come on," Bonnie said, pulling at my hand, hoisting herself up out of her chair.

She stood and led me, slowly and limply, the twenty yards to light pole forty-five, beneath which was the water, not the tip of Marin County.

She placed her hand on the railing, which, I realized at that moment, was vaguely the color of her former hair. She put her other hand on my shoulder.

"Now help me up here," she said.

I didn't think. I just crouched and made a step with my interlocked hands. Bonnie placed her foot into them and I lifted my arms up. She hardly weighed anything.

Together, we were able to get her up so that she stood on the railing, albeit unsteadily, swaying dangerously backward. From behind, I held onto her hips to keep her from falling.

"Hey! What the hell!" someone yelled.

"Get her down from there!" another shouted.

I glanced over my shoulder. Three people were sprinting towards us, as if on Bridge Duty. They were by light pole forty-nine some forty yards away.

"Are you sure you want to do this?" I asked.

Bonnie nodded.

She spread her arms and leaned her head back, her face basking in the sun's rays.

The trio of strangers were closing in on us, the scampering of their feet against the concrete growing closer and closer.

Bonnie crouched slightly, gathering strength in her legs, and I felt her lunge forward.

But I pulled her back. I couldn't do it. Selfishly, I knew I couldn't live with myself if I allowed it.

We fell backwards onto the pavement, Bonnie landing safely on top of me.

The three strangers, two men and a woman, reached us in a swirl of panic.

"Are you okay?" the woman said.

"Jesus, what were you thinking?" one man asked. "You almost Jumped!"

I stood and waved them off.

"Please," I said. "It's okay now. Just leave us be."

"What the hell, man?" the other man said. "Were you trying to kill her?"

"No. Look," I said, pointing at Bonnie, "she's sick. I need to get her home. I'm sorry to trouble you. Please, just leave us alone now."

Reluctantly, they left, glancing over their shoulders several times.

Bonnie lay on the pavement, crying.

"I'm sorry," I said. "I couldn't do it."

I crouched next to her and held her. She punched my arm and said, "You bastard! Why did you do that?" I let her hit me and cry for as long as it took.

When she was done, I helped her up and we looked out over the bridge's east end. The sun was just beginning to set and the outskirts of the city spilled over the rolling coastal hills like a solidified frosting.

"I want to go back to the hospital now," said Bonnie.

She took my hand and together we walked to the Helen Diller Cancer Center on Divisadero Street where, a few months later, she would die. I got to be there for that, at the side of her bed, with Beth Fuller, Fiona Struthers, Chris Swinton, and the others.

I still think about Bonnie. I think about her a lot. It's mostly during practice that I think of her, when I'm doing the poses: eagle, dolphin, crow, side angle, warrior, tree, standing-mountain backbend. Bridge.

BROKEN VESSEL

IN THE MORNINGS, WHEN Sally helped her mother Esther get dressed, Esther would insist on having a pair of her husband Gary's blue jeans and a flannel button-up laid out on the bed. At the breakfast table, a third bowl of oatmeal was placed, heated and stirred with cinnamon, at the spot Sally's father would have sat had he not been dead some six years.

It was the same in any number of other ways. A third, unused blue toothbrush accompanied Sally's and Esther's on the bathroom sink. A new recliner had been purchased, placed off to the right of the television in the approximate spot her father's La-Z-Boy had been in the old house. On trips to the doctor's office or the grocery store, Esther insisted on riding in the backseat so that her dead husband could sit passenger. Of course, it went without saying, at lunch and supper, he had a plate of whatever Sally and Esther were having.

At first, the doctor had encouraged Sally to indulge Esther's delusions. It would, after all, provide some comfort. But once Esther began having bits of conversation with Gary, the doctor had changed his story. "You might have to start thinking about a place for her," he told Sally at the last visit. Just this past Sunday, Esther had snapped at a nice young man at church, ordering him to scoot down the pew so that Gary had a place to sit.

Sally met her brother Jim at a coffee shop a block from her apartment. He gave his opinion this way, "I don't think it's safe to leave her alone right now, even when we're a block away."

Sally stirred some raw sugar into her café latte. Outside, the snowy tail end of a Minnesota winter—it was early March now—clung sporadically to Minneapolis's buildings and sidewalks, the city's many yet-to-bloom deciduous trees still bearing frost upon their branches. That day's *Star Tribune* lay between them on the table, the corner of the front page bearing the headline "Paul Bunyan Strikes Again" in reference to the bearded serial bank robber who favored flannel button-ups and stocking caps. This time, the paper said, he hit the Sunrise Bank on Blaisdell Avenue for $1,343, once again foiling authorities by temporarily attaching a stolen license plate to his car. They'd tracked the plates to an old man in St. Anthony who had been watching the Golden Gophers game in his living room at the time of the robbery, and still was when authorities pulled up to his house.

"She can still cook for herself," Sally said. "Granted, she needs a bit of help bathing and getting dressed. And I lay her pills out for her each morning."

"But the talking," Jim said. "Remember the other day when I took her and Julie to the park? I mean, she used to love playing with Julie. Pushing her on the swing or catching her at the bottom of the slide. But she just stood there talking to *him* the whole time. She kept pointing at the skyline and talking about the '60s."

The spring couldn't get here soon enough, as far as Sally was concerned. The streets and sidewalks would be cleared, much more navigable. It was dangerous zipping around on snow and ice.

"Well I don't know if we can afford to put her in a home," Sally said. Jim opened his mouth to speak, but Sally went on, "And before you even suggest it, we're *not* putting her in one of those state-run places. I read all about the abuses. They treat the inmates at Hennepin County better than they do the folks at those state-run places."

Jim shook his head. He'd be forty-four next year and had no money to speak of, Sally knew. He and his wife worked at the same call center, made enough to cover bills and a birthday and Christmas present for Julie, their three-year-old.

"I might be getting a promotion, though," Sally lied. "Warehouse manager."

Jim thought Sally loaded boxes of frozen beef patties into semis for a temp agency. It was partly true. Her name was on the call list at Aventure Staffing. And sometimes she worked a day or two at a warehouse. But not lately.

"You've been saying that for a year now," Jim said. "And warehouse wages aren't enough to cover the cost of one of them nice places you want to put her in. Manager or not."

"No," Sally admitted. "But it's something."

The flannel shirts and blue jeans had belonged to Sally's father. Esther had brought them when she'd moved into Sally's apartment some two years prior, the cracking of her mind then in its beginning stages. They were right there in the second drawer of the faux wood dresser next to Esther's bed, and so the disguise had occurred to Sally as a natural extension of the idea itself. After all, Esther's many medications—ACE inhibitors, diuretics, beta blockers, analgesics, anti-inflammatories, muscle relaxers—were quite expensive when taken together.

It came to Sally out of her own past, because she'd done it before—twice, though not with banks. At sixteen, she'd dropped out of high school, and at nineteen, she was with a man who worked at a gas station. She thought: wouldn't it be funny if I wore a mask and came in one night while you were working and you gave me all the money in the till? And so they did it, mostly for fun. They blew the $162 the next night hopping around to various bars.

A year later, when they were desperate, they did it again,

for only \$112. But he was stupid and had smoked a joint by the dumpster out back on one of his breaks. The manager saw it on the security footage and fired him on the spot.

"I needed to calm down," he pleaded to Sally.

But she left him and somehow, twenty years passed. She'd waited tables off and on, tried telemarketing. Twice, she'd come close to being married. When her father died, she felt an innate responsibility to care for her mother, almost like a calling. Through Esther's slow decline, Sally's life finally seemed to center itself upon something meaningful.

And now, after almost a year of doing it once each month, the disguise was a routine. She wrapped a small blanket around herself to thicken her torso, then donned her father's flannel shirt. With the aid of a belt, the Wrangler jeans held snug to her waist. She wore an old pair of her father's workmen's boots. She attached the fake beard, brown and thick like her father's. She wore leather gloves, a stocking hat, and large aviator sunglasses that covered a good deal of her face.

She could do the whole thing in under sixty seconds. Most amateurs were desperate and reckless. They barreled into the bank, shouting orders like they were in a movie. They spun in circles, looking for cops and security guards, pointed their guns at customers or tellers whom they suspected of reaching for their phones. They grabbed the money greedily, not even bothering to check for marked bills or dye packs. They plowed through bystanders on their way to the door. They sped off, running red lights and leaving skid marks.

Not Sally. She never used a gun. She calmly informed the teller this was a bank robbery, requested only clean bills. Dumbfounded, the teller handed her the money, which Sally stuffed in her saddlebag. Then she walked out, got in her car, and drove back home to Esther—stopping at red lights and staying under the speed limit.

The knock on Sally's door came at three in the morning. She hurried out of bed to answer it, not wanting Esther to be woken.

It was Jim.

"It's mom," he said. "You need to come with me to University Hospital."

"What?" Sally said, confused. "She went to bed at nine."

"She got up," Jim said. "And she took your car."

Sally craned her neck, peering back at the bedroom hallway. How had she not heard Esther?

"Give me a second," Sally said.

She went back to her bedroom and pulled on one of the stocking hats. She grabbed her parka from the coat rack by the door. On the way to the hospital, Jim explained that Esther had taken Sally's car down 1st Avenue to Nicollet Island. That Esther was standing at the bank of the Mississippi when a cop happened to pull up.

"She was going to walk into the river," Jim said.

"No," Sally said. "There's those benches by the pavilion. She and dad would go and sit there."

"She wasn't on the benches," Jim said. "She was by the water."

In the hospital bed, Esther, who had worn no coat during the late-night excursion, looked as if her slumbering head were unattached to her body, so thoroughly had they wrapped her in warm blankets.

Sally paid minimal attention as the doctor, a resident at the University no older than thirty, encouraged them to seek out "greater supervision" for Esther. Instead, Sally focused on the doctor's youthful face, how her forehead and cheeks, smooth and unlined as marble, belonged more appropriately on a grade school teacher who helped children broach the world than on an ER doctor who treated disintegrating bodies in the twilight of cold winter nights. That face, so soft, made Sally feel, at forty-five, as if her life had passed her by. She saw a blurry alternative path behind her, one she should've taken many years ago. It emerged somewhere similar to where this doctor had been led.

They would keep Esther overnight, the doctor said before she left.

When it was just the two of them with their mother, Jim shrugged and said, "I guess this is it."

Sally wondered if she could change the locks on her door to prevent Esther from escaping. Or perhaps use one of those baby monitors to keep a closer eye on her. She stopped at the thought of putting a lock on Esther's door, realizing no matter what route they went, Esther was a prisoner.

Three thousand eight hundred and twenty-six dollars. That's how much it cost per month to house Esther in private care at Sunrise Community Center. And that was the cheapest in town. Sally had argued with Jim the next morning right there in the kitchen over where to put Esther, while Esther herself, oblivious, sat on the couch watching *Judge Judy* not fifteen feet away. It was like she was an old pet, unaware that her fate teetered in the balance of a sibling squabble.

Eventually, Jim caved when Sally threatened to drive down to Sunrise this instant and pay for a two-month stay in advance.

"That's like eight thousand dollars," Jim said, shocked.

"I have some in savings."

In truth, it was stashed in her closet. Close to nine thousand dollars.

Jim studied Sally in disbelief, as if waiting for her to admit she was bluffing. "Well what happens after two months?" Jim asked. "Do we just let her get evicted?"

Social Services would step in, Sally knew, and lock Esther up in what Sally imagined was some kind of medieval dungeon.

"I'll come up with the money," Sally said.

"Where? Where are you going to come up with an extra four grand a month?"

"I'll get the money," Sally snapped.

Immediately, she regretted her tone. Jim looked hurt, almost scared, like Sally was about to draw a gun.

On the television, Judge Judy chastised an adulterous husband. "Don't pee on my leg and tell me it's raining," she said.

They told Esther they were taking her to a restaurant that happened to be in a hotel. This was Jim's idea, because the first thing you saw when you walked into Sunrise Community Center was the cafeteria to your right.

"Then we take her to her room and just kind of leave her there," Jim said.

Like a friendly kidnapping, Sally thought. Or a hunting trip one never returns from.

Jim drove, while Sally sat in back with Esther. Dead Gary sat passenger. Esther talked to him intermittently, pointing out the bright afternoon sun, how the temperature surely had climbed to over forty degrees by now. On KMOJ 89.3, they announced Paul Bunyan had hit the Stonebridge Bank on Washington Avenue that very morning for $1,114. This time, the license plates, spotted by a customer, were traced to an older couple out in Falcon Heights.

Inside, Sunrise looked like it did on its website: tiled floors and flower-patterned walls soaked in fluorescent lights. In the cafeteria to the right, a few lifeless bodies, mostly women, slumped over their trays. They didn't seem to be eating. Off to the left, past the reception desk, a few more residents sat about in a living room area. There was a wood table, some cushioned chairs, and an artificial ficus tree. One man had a book in his lap, though he stared straight forward.

"We just need to go back to the waiting room," Jim said. "And they'll come get us when our table is ready."

It went smoothly until they got to the room. Beige carpeted, furnished with a soft loveseat, and equipped with a large window offering a view of Balsam fir pines and the sky, it was a nice room by nursing home standards. But the room wasn't why things fell apart.

"Gary? Where's Gary?" Esther asked, panic enveloping her tone. "Where did Gary go?"

"He's right here," Jim assumed. "Isn't he?"

"Where's Gary?"

In a matter of seconds, Esther grew hysterical. She shrieked horrifically and pleaded not to be left alone in this place. She pulled at the sides of her fluffy white hair.

"You'd rather see me die!" Esther screamed.

Two staff appeared, a middle-aged man and a young woman. They pushed their way past Sally and Jim. The man gripped Esther's forearm, forced her down on the loveseat.

"Careful," Sally said.

"It's okay," the man said. "It's okay."

Esther continued demanding to know Gary's whereabouts. The man continued to say that it was okay. The young woman ushered Jim and Sally from the room.

It happened so fast.

Suddenly, they were in the hallway. The door was shut. The screams were muffled. The nameplate on the door still bore the name of the previous occupant.

A man: Frederick Burns.

Directly across the hall, a woman stood in her open doorway with the aid of her walker. Sliced tennis balls cupped the base of each of its four legs. Her jaw moved frantically up and down, like she was chewing something for dear life.

That first night by herself, Sally heated up a bowl of leftover goulash, then watched part of a TV nature documentary about bioluminescent deep sea organisms. She tried not to think of Esther. But while glowing squids and neon fish danced across the screen, all Sally could imagine was what Esther was doing in her little room, how they were treating her, whether she'd had enough to eat.

Sally and Jim visited every day of Esther's first week. It was ugly each time, with Esther accusing them of leaving her in this place, which was true. She also blamed them for taking Gary from her. There was no way of knowing if this was true. In her isolation, Esther broke things—dishes, a flowerpot, her own window—and these damages were tacked on to her bill.

The nights alone ran together for Sally, the only differences among them being the organisms on the television screen and Sally's belief that the lights in the apartment were growing progressively dimmer. The whole place, it seemed, was a burning candle in its waning stages.

As Sally sat before the television, the phantom presence of her mother loomed all around, felt but not seen, her figure somewhere just beyond Sally's periphery. But as the night wore on, Sally started to worry Esther had been in a car accident or had taken drugs or was alone with a boy—whatever monstrosity it was parents feared most.

Finally, Sally couldn't help it. She was certain that if she just checked Esther's bedroom, she'd find her there, either sleeping or rereading some passage from Ecclesiastes. When she did, however, the room was empty, the bed neatly made and the shades drawn. Sally shut the door and lie on the bed, imagining she was Esther and that she could hear herself out in the kitchen, fixing supper or jangling keys on her way out the door. She thought of the Mississippi, not a mile away, and wondered how often Esther had laid in this very spot and contemplated her escape. Perhaps it was not a question of whether or not to do it, but of waiting for the right moment.

Sally turned her attention to the window. Something passed before the shades. A specter, silhouetted by the ivory linen. Sally decided it was Gary, her father, for she felt him there anyway. Not as palpably as she felt Esther, but still there all the same: his toothbrush, which remained on the bathroom sink; his recliner chair, which Sally sometimes sat in for the heck of it; his place at the table, as well as Esther's, which Sally continued to set; and his clothes, which Sally continued to wear.

Alone and with no one to see her, Sally pulled on the Wrangler jeans and the flannel button-up. She attached the beard. She walked about the apartment, casually as you like.

Standing in front of her bathroom mirror, she felt oddly complete. As if, at least in this moment, they could all be together if she wanted them to be.

"Hello, Gary," Sally said.

"Hello," said Gary.

You couldn't lock the doors at Sunrise, but you could at least shut them for privacy, which is what Sally did when she entered Esther's room. She already had on the Wrangler jeans and boots. The rest she toted in her saddlebag.

"What are you doing here?" Esther asked.

On the television, canned laughter filled a brief silence. Sally hadn't planned on what she would say.

"Have you seen dad?"

Esther turned away from Sally, faced the TV.

"Don't talk to me about him," Esther said.

Esther had reached her breaking point with Sally and Jim, asking them not to visit her until they brought Gary back to her. Or, conversely, until she returned to Gary.

"Can I use your bathroom?"

Esther pointed in the direction of her little bathroom, which was adjacent to her bed. Sally entered and shut the door. Inside, attached the beard. She parted her hair at the side the way she remembered her father doing. She wrapped a towel around her belly, then buttoned up the flannel. She wondered: will she recognize him so much younger? And she knew that Esther would, that there was simply no mistaking him.

She studied herself in the mirror, now fully changed. The last thing he had said to her was that the Twins needed a first baseman who could hit home runs. He'd said this so casually because, like everyone else, he had no idea that an artery would burst in his brain the very next day, that he would hemorrhage out of this life within eight hours of the broken vessel.

Sally took the first baseman comment and from there, channeled the rest of his voice, his warm auditory hues, his smooth baritone. As her father, he was a man whose presence had never left her.

"Hello," Sally said into the mirror.

A vocal match. And a spitting image to boot.

Sally knew that she not only could give this to Esther, but that she should. In a way, it was like this was the disguise's higher purpose, that all along, its intention was not to conceal, but to manifest.

Sally took one last look at herself, then left.

She approached Esther on the couch.

Her mother looked at him.

Went to the well one too many times. That's what the *Star Tribune* said. Which was one way of looking at it. Normally, Sally would wait a month in between banks. You didn't want to push it. Instead, she was going weekly, and in that sense, religiously. To name a few: a Wells Fargo near Northeast Park. A Woodlands National off Stevens Square.

But really, it was the fact that she'd decided to hit two in one day that did her in. Though it could not be said to be a real decision on Sally's part, not in the sense that one gives thought to one's options and outcomes. It was automatic, as if Sally were delivering mail from one stop to the next. She simply drove off from Park State Bank near Nicollet Mall, $2,084 in her saddlebag, and the next thing she knew, she was parked in front of the Bremer Bank in Lyn-Lake.

At the counter, she informed the teller of the situation, the stipulation of clean bills. Stunned, the teller, a baby-faced young man with a fohawk, handed over stacks of cash, which Sally slid into her saddlebag. Someone had spotted the license plate at the last bank. Cops were on the lookout. Sally coolly walked out, loot in tow. She heard someone say, "That's Paul Bunyan."

She was a block from her apartment when the red and blue lights appeared in her rearview. Even in the daylight, they had an uncanny brightness about them, like lighthouse beams.

You'd think it would be the gun pulled on her. Or the sting of pavement against her cheek after she was pinned to the ground. Or the cuffing. Or the ride. Or the fingerprinting. Or the clank of the cell door.

But the worst part was the siren. It immediately recalled the shrillness of Esther's scream. It had been weeks since Sally heard it—she had not been back to Sunrise since—but it was right there, a voice directly into her ear.

"Ghost!"

"No, it's me, Gary," Sally said in her father's voice. "It's me." Sally thought: just look at me. Can't you tell?

But Esther kept shouting ghost, and she kept screaming in what can only be described as a primal cry for help.

And Esther kept screaming even after the staff rushed in, even after Sally had removed the beard and said, "It's just me. It's Sally."

Ghost.

She aged ten years in ten months, her scalp littered with greys. Bags hung beneath her eyes. Her cheeks sagged. Her back hunched a bit without her hunching it. Her fingers curled a bit without her curling them.

Esther was at times close by: in Sally's cell, in her mind, in the head of the mop. And for that matter, so was Gary: in the corners of rooms, on her fingernails and eyelids, at the edges of things. The two of them flittered in and out like thoughts, rose and fell like the tide. Occasionally, Sally resisted the urge to speak to them aloud. Occasionally, she didn't.

A year and a half in, Jim visited one morning at the correctional facility in Shakopee to tell her that it was done, Esther had passed peacefully the night before. Sally suspected foul play on the part of Social Services, but she did not voice this view.

The day of the funeral, Sally mopped the cafeteria after breakfast. She did this three times a week for four years. Then she read part of a Louis L'Amour novel. Half the library, it seemed, consisted of Louis L'Amour and Danielle Steele. After lunch, she attended her job training course, where she was learning how to weld. That day, they continued practicing their TIG arc welds on the seals of old jet engines. Next week, they would move on to building up saw blades. Late afternoon, she met with Dr. Lisa Knutson, her counselor. She talked about how she missed Esther and Gary and Jim, how she hated herself for not being able to attend the funeral. Then she broke down, sobbed for five uninterrupted minutes. When she was done, Dr. Knutson told her not to be too hard on herself and to focus on the good things she'd done for Esther. This was the height of wisdom in terms of free prison counseling. At supper, she ate runza casserole with Rhonda and Beatrice, two women in their sixties who never said anything to anyone. At night, she read a bit more of L'Amour. She said goodnight to Tamara, her cellmate, and went to sleep.

In this way, she passed four years, a lenient sentence earned by her lack of priors and her never having used a gun. She got her welding certification and had a job lined up with a local company who took chances on ex-cons. Insofar that it was spring in Minneapolis, the day she got out was like the day she went in. Only the two days were nothing alike. After soaking in fluorescent light for four years, all the ways in which you'd expect the physical appearance of the world to shine shone all the more for her absence.

The trees were greener. The sun was brighter. The skyline somehow more vibrant. The sensation of air crisp and beyond fresh.

She made Jim take her to St. Anthony's Cemetery so that she could see Esther's name alongside Gary's. They passed a few of the banks she'd robbed, and she knew Jim was made uncomfortable by this, could feel the elevated tension coming from him, the weird burden she had become to him. No one had her for a sister except Jim, and Jim she appreciated all the more for leaving it unsaid.

Then they drove to Jim's one-bedroom apartment where she would be allowed to sleep on the couch in the living room. She didn't want to impose, but Jim assured her, after his wife had left and taken Julie, who was now eight, he could use the company.

That night, her first one free, she lay on the couch and contemplated doing what Esther had done. She saw herself sneaking out and taking Jim's car down 1st Avenue to Nicollet Island. There, she would sit on a bench, alone. She would gaze into the star-speckled black sky, breathe the crisp night air, and listen to the flowing river.

Instead, she lay still. Slits of streetlight arranged themselves neatly on the floor of the dark apartment, like white steps. Their specters moved about in the recesses light did not reach, and also in the light itself. Like always, she saw them, and like always, they saw her. No love worth its salt allowed one to forget.

She turned over, away from them. She shut her eyes. She had work in the morning.

YEAR OF OUR LAWN

It was the beginning of spring, the time when our lawns came to life. We planted our flowers, tended to our bushes, sprinkled Miracle-Gro on our grass. We waved to our neighbors in the mornings, commented politely on their floral handiwork whether we thought it pleasing or not. For example, "My, Frank, your hydrangeas are coming in nicely this year." Or, "Gee, Gloria, your tulips look better and better every year." In our town, we took great pride in our lawns. We always had.

That year, Diane and Rick Porter started a lawn embellishment trend the likes of which our town had never seen. The Porters cared deeply about lawn ornamentation, had always been our town's trendsetters. In the '80s, as a young couple just married, they'd been the first to put pink flamingoes on their lawn. In the '90s, they started the lawn gnome renaissance. Into the 21st century, Diane had flown the Burmese and Nepalese flags as vague political statements we never quite understood, while Rick worked tirelessly to grow the greenest grass. "Pebble Beach fairway quality," he liked to brag.

We weren't surprised when a white tent appeared in their yard, the kind you might see at a county fair. For one whole day, unseen workers toiled inside the tent, their secret work obscured from our view. The suspense was unbearable.

The next day, we gathered in front of the Porters' for the unveiling. The tent was gone and a white sheet cloaked the lawn's lumpy centerpiece, which stood about six feet in height, some fifteen in length. Diane Porter herself stood next to it at one end, holding the sheet's edge.

"Count down from three!" she shouted. She held up three fingers. We chanted in unison. On one, Diane let her rip. The white sheet fluttered down in waves, its movements the sound of flapping wings.

At first, we were confused, unsure what to make of the restaurant scene in which six animal couples—two white-tailed deer, two black bears, and two foxes—sat at three separate tables, while nearby, one bipedal Shetland pony held a steak platter.

It quickly came into focus. We recognized the multicolored summer dresses and Western plaid button-ups as those fashions in vogue in our town, and of course, the trademark white apron and bifocals worn by the Shetland, who was the anthropomorphic embodiment of Jody Howard, the short, portly proprietor of Jody's Steakhouse, our town's most popular restaurant.

"It's Jody!" someone shouted, pointing at the Shetland.

"And that's me and Gina!" said Dan Foals, pointing at the attractive young deer couple.

We identified the black bears as Greg and Bonnie Shedd, two of Jody's most prominent patrons, and the fox couple as the animal simulacra of the Porters themselves.

We clapped. We whistled. We shook the Porters' hands, patted their backs, told them how lovely it all was. To be sure—and this is something so typical of the Porters—it was a definitive advancement in lawn embellishment, a truly historical day in our town.

Though we did not yet fully understand the relationship between ourselves and the animal facsimiles, there was something immediately satisfying in viewing some essential aspect of our town brought to life. It was as if we were watching ourselves on television, or viewing a movie about our town, albeit one acted out by animals. The Foals and Shedds could point at the deer and the black bears and say, "That's us!" And all the while as we cheered, in our own heads, we envisioned our own yards, imagined what animals and what scenes would look best brought to life on our own lawns.

Someone was bound to make the first move.

The white tent next appeared in the yard of George and Kim Strom. It was there for three whole days, which built a restless excitement among us. We needed to see what was next, needed to know so we could figure out how best to respond. George and Kim owned the insurance office uptown, and they were famous for trading in their car every year, sometimes twice, for something new, something shinier.

At the Stroms' unveiling, the lawn's centerpiece, this one even bigger, was again cloaked in a large white sheet. Like Diane, George Strom, on the count of three, whipped the sheet away, like a matador fooling a charging bull.

Immediately, we were struck by the sheer number of animals—thirteen in all, among them goats, possums, raccoons, and sheep—as well as the more elaborate use of props. It was a scene from the drugstore on Main Street. There were two long shelves stocked full of medicinal packages, pill bottles, and knick-knacks. The animals stood in a line in between the shelves leading to the counter where our town's pharmacist, Brad Callahan, represented as a badger, stood waiting as he did six days a week to fill our prescriptions.

We erupted in applause, cheered the way we did Friday nights for the high school football team. George and Kim joined hands and took a bow in front of the animals.

Later, we walked around our own blocks, reluctant to return to our own yards, which seemed suddenly barren, woefully inadequate, bereft of spectacle. What good was a porch, a swing, a maple tree, without also a taxidermied drugstore scene, or some other such pageantry? How could we ever look upon our own lawns with pride after having seen what we'd just seen, not once, but twice?

The Rosenbaums were next, and they raised the bar higher, taking advantage of the mysterious shop's premium options, available to customers willing to pay extra. The workers labored in the white tent for seven days. The emerging scene was so large they had to drape white sheets over individual pieces as they were finished. In one week, the entirety of the Rosenbaum's yard was converted into a live action scene of our little municipal park.

Some twenty-five animals, adults and adolescents alike, swung on swing sets, teeter-tottered, slid down slides, climbed the jungle gym, flew kites, and dug in the sand. Two little boys, recognizing themselves as fox pup facsimiles, ran from the crowd to the jungle gym to play. Other children joined in, and we spent the rest of the afternoon as if we were actually at the park, strolling about the grounds, picnicking, napping in the sun. Those of us with facsimiles felt a special joy, as if we were having twice the fun, ourselves and our taxidermied counterparts.

The Andersons, the Fowlers, and the Kaisers, all next in line, created increasingly elaborate scenes of, respectively, our public library, the inside of our county courthouse, and the baseball field, each furbished with more detailed props and sets and populated with greater numbers of animal townspeople. A growing sense of wonder accompanied each new scene, as if seeing ourselves living our lives as animals revealed some previously unknown truth of our town, though we couldn't quite place our collective finger on the nature of that truth.

Some thought the scenes revealed, beyond the love we held for our lawns, our town's deep, abiding sense of community, since the trend seemed to be moving towards recreating every scene of our town, which by its nature inhered a spirit of inclusion. Imitation is the sincerest form of flattery, this argument went, and we loved our town so much that we were building a second one. And what better place to erect such a tribute than on that most hallowed of our town's institutions, our front lawns?

But there was a counterpoint to this interpretation, one that argued the lawn scenes revealed a darker, more unsettling truth, one that pointed towards a deep-seated division. For one, not everyone had an animal facsimile. Instead of seeing the hidden wonders in the lawn scenes, they saw only their own conspicuous absence, as if by their anthropomorphic exclusion, they weren't really a part of our town.

Almost instinctually, without our meaning to, we treated them differently, the un-taxidermied. If they sat by us in church or in the bleachers on Friday nights, we scooted over, created distance. If we passed by them on the sidewalks or in the grocery store, we looked away, covered our children's eyes, for with no facsimile, it was as if they were without identity, just unwanted strangers.

Moreover, there were those who objected to their assigned facsimiles. People such as Brad Callahan, who questioned what insinuations the Stroms were making by portraying him as a badger pharmacist. And Tessie Hodges, who demanded that her ex-husband remove her cow facsimile from his lawn scene. And the Fosters who, just because they used baby straps, felt it unfair to be depicted by the O'Briens as kangaroos with protruding joey heads. It was as if people were saying through their lawn scenes what they really felt about one another, that the lawn scenes were bringing to the surface a surreptitious bitterness that had always been there.

There was also the question of money, which not everyone possessed in equal measure. Some of modest means, such as the Jeffreys, sold their new 4x4 pickup to satisfy the taxidermist bill, so that they could display in their lawn a scene from our town's bank, wherein a coyote facsimile of Gill Jeffrey himself withdrew a large sum of Monopoly play money. It was the first such scene in which the creator overtly depicted an idealized version of life in our town, one beyond the reach, at least for some, of the current reality.

Others, such as the Crenshaws and Boltons, pooled their money to afford a scene of our town's dollar store, which straddled equally the border of their lawns. Oddly, the shelves in the scene featured only name-brand products, an inaccuracy we read as wish fulfillment.

Some stooped to more dubious means. It was rumored, though never proven, the Foltzes used Derek Jr.'s student loan refund to cover expenses on their scene of our town's country club, a membership to which the Foltzes could never afford.

And even as the white tent moved from lawn to lawn, as summer took hold with its golden rays and brightened our town like luminous stage lights, there were those who would never be able to afford a customized lawn scene. Instead, they threw themselves into the now old-fashioned form of lawn enhancement. They tore out whole beds of flowers, planted them anew with more exotic, more colorful ones. They mowed every day instead of every five days. They sprinkled twice the amount of Miracle-Gro, toiling like peasants in scorching fields. They researched micronutrients in soil, minerals in rainwater, optimum durations of sunlight—anything to give themselves an edge, anything within their means to make them feel as if they were a part of things. And those of the highest means, the most well-to-do, as if to throw salt in the wounds, pushed for a city ordinance requiring the display of a taxidermied lawn scene, which had quickly become the new lawn standard. Which of course raised the question that if a family could not afford a taxidermied lawn scene, would our town provide them one?

It also became abundantly clear that the lawn scenes, as much fascination as they evoked, as much as they united us in wonder, were encouraging a kind of excess that bordered on pomposity. For example, Vivian Miller, our town's mayor, produced in her lawn a scene of her office in city hall, twice the stature of its actual size. Instead of the demure faux wood floors and walls of her actual

office, the one in her lawn bore red velvet, gold-trimmed walls and
a marble floor, resembling more closely a queen's throne room
than a municipal public servant's office. For her own facsimile she
chose the apex predator lion, which admittedly did not surprise us,
given the overinflated sense of her own importance as mayor, a job
no one else wanted.

Or take Pastor Ike Bradley, who went so far as to demolish his
own garage and one-quarter of his home's easternmost section to
make room for a scene of our town's Methodist sanctuary, which
housed at least thirty more facsimile parishioners than actually
attended his Sunday services.

No one took it as far as the Briggses. They built an anthropomorphic recreation of our town's single largest event, the annual
homecoming parade, complete with the students' pirate-themed
floats, the automobiles containing the homecoming royalty, the
entire high school band, and crowds of spectators along both sides
of the street. The display spilled over their front lawn and into the
street, wrapped all the way around the surrounding three blocks,
impeding traffic and pedestrians alike. At summer's end, when our
town's actual homecoming parade marched, most instead attended
the omnipresent Briggs' animal parade. After all, the Briggs' parade
was bigger, more visually stunning. The band's uniforms were
nicer, their instruments shinier. The floats were grander, the cars
fancier, the spirit of it all more robust.

We encouraged it, this bawdiness, for beyond the lawn scenes'
philosophical revelations, beyond their ability to teach us things
about ourselves, the scenes filled us with a compulsive urge for
more. We felt a persistent, obsessive craving for the surpassing of
whatever elusive standard we imagined had been created. It was as
if the lawn scenes possessed a will independent of our power, like
robots who evolve consciousness, like the mutant miscreation that
seeks to conquer its maker.

It all started to fall apart in autumn once we ran out of scenes. We had completed on our lawns the anthropomorphic second town. At first we felt a deep sense of calmness, as if we'd finished some protracted, strenuous journey. For a while, we moved seamlessly in and out of our real and facsimiled lives, feeling as if, at long last, our town was now twice as good as it used to be, our marriages and friendships twice as strong, our lives twice as happy.

But an unease set in. Our children had stopped swimming in the Le Croixs' facsimile community swimming pool, had stopped playing baseball games on the Dickersons' facsimile field. By the time autumn's chill set in, the Rosenbaums' facsimile municipal park contained only animals, their hooves and paws covered in small piles of red, yellow, and brown deciduous leaves.

The much more salient problem, the one that, looking back, signaled the beginning of the end, was our collective feeling as if there was something more, that we could go further, that there was still some taxidermic summit we had not yet reached. Though initially only privately, we wondered with increasing agitation: Is this all there is? The protestors began vandalizing some of the facsimiles, which we left spray-painted or dismembered, for an abiding disappointment took hold of us, rendered us indifferent to the maintenance of our second town, as if it deserved to be defaced for failing to fulfill us.

We knew that something had to be done, and there were those who thought the solution was to build yet another town. They proposed erecting a larger third town beyond the city limits of the first town, using only nature's largest specimens such as giraffes, rhinoceroses, elephants, possibly even whales. Conversely there were those who advocated constructing a miniaturized third town on the lawns of the taxidermied second town, using nature's smallest specimens such as mice, hummingbirds, tiny lizards, possibly even insects. Moreover, the argument went, we could build a microscopic fourth town, using only single-celled organisms, possibly even viruses.

These arguments never truly gained any traction, for beyond our inability to reach a consensus, there was also the beleaguering slippery slope of just how many towns was enough. If four, why not five? If five, why not six? Regardless of how many towns we could reproduce, would we not, in the end, feel the same dissatisfaction, the same disappointed yearning that currently plagued us?

We turned to the only people who could help, those whose consistent visionary lawn embellishment had gotten us this far.

The Porters' solution was remarkably simple. When the next fashionable step forward is unclear, they explained, the answer is to go backward, though their special term for it was *retro*.

Following the Porters' lead, we altered our lawn scenes to evoke the '90s. We clothed our facsimiles in pastel-patterned swishy suits, knee-torn jeans, flannel button-ups, high-waisted jean shorts, Doc Martens. Of course, we also brought back the lawn gnomes.

For one ephemeral week towards the end of autumn, just before the first frost set in, it worked. We were calmed by the alterations, our appetites temporarily satisfied. Some went so far as to pretend as if it really were the '90s, asking one another, in casual conversation, if they had seen the new *Seinfeld* episode or heard the latest military developments in the Persian Gulf.

We should have seen it coming, the imminent, inevitable one-upmanship, should have known the '90s would not deliver us from ourselves. One morning we awoke to find the Stroms had taken their lawn a step further, raised the bar one decade to the '80s, the era of big hair, pastel leg warmers over black tights, mullets, and pink flamingo lawn ornaments.

It set the whole thing into motion again. The Rosenbaums transported their lawn, through bell-bottomed pants and tie-dye T-shirts and miscellaneous acoustic guitars, to the '70s. To which the Andersons, the Fowlers, and the Kaisers all responded by pushing their scenes back one decade apiece, into the '60s, the '50s, and the '40s, each lawn more historically detailed and evocative than that which preceded it, each earlier decade one in which our town had fewer and fewer residents.

The fervor for our taxidermied historical lawn scenes took on a new urgency as the first frost set in. We came to believe that by moving backwards, we would find what we were looking for, the elusive truth in the lawn scenes we had at times grazed with our fingertips but had remained beyond our collective reach. We believed, with each generational step back, the answer would be there, appear perhaps vividly, perhaps fleetingly in the scenes, the reason why we were doing it—as it were, the ultimate mystery of our town.

Winter loomed, the first snowfall imminent, its white blankets threatening to cloak our lawns like a sheet cast over an expired body. The De La Croixs and the Dickersons moved us back faster into the '30s, '20s. The number of us who could verify our lawn scenes' historical accuracies shrunk to a handful until, by the 1910s, there were none left.

But we knew our town began in 1859, and that if we could get back there, to the very beginning of it all, perhaps that's where the answer lay.

So we did our best. We set aside differences, worked together. We clothed the animals in grey pioneer dresses and fluffy white button-ups and suspenders. We dug up sod huts, built clunky wagons. We made it all the way back to 1859, to the founding of our town, when one family of pioneers first stopped their wagon along the bumpy prairie and said, "This place is as good as any."

When the pioneer town was finished—indeed, the original version of our town—we collapsed, exhausted, ashamed at our foolishness. Given how far we'd taken it, some of us laughed, amused that we had ever thought there would be more truth in lawn scenes from 1859 than there were in the present day. Some even questioned whether there had ever been any truth in the lawn scenes at all, or if they had just been another peculiar mania to grip our town's quenchless thirst for imagined chic.

As the snow began to fall in thick, wet chunks, we decided to create one final scene. Only half-jokingly did we refer to it as the final reveal.

We knocked down the sod huts in our lawns. We removed any and all props, stuffed them in our garages. We stripped the animals of any clothing. Each of us carried one to the open prairie outside of town, to the liminal space between the edge of our township and the fringes of the hilly woodlands.

Here, there were no houses, no cars, no streets. The snow draped trees in white balls, covered the ground and the brush in powdered layers. We could feel the biting winter breeze more acutely here. We set the animals down, backed away, and gazed.

For a moment, they seemed to come to life, a sudden vitality materializing as they stood in their habitat. This was our town before it was a town: a snow-covered wilderness.

We glanced uneasily at one another. Did we really belong here? Should we, like our ancestors, pack the family in a wagon and head west? Is this what our lawns had been trying to tell us?

The temperature continued to drop. The bitter wind picked up. The snow fell more thickly. For a while, we huddled together, a herd seeking warmth. Against the elements, we did not stand a chance, yet we were one.

It soon grew too cold, the wind too strong. We shuffled off to our heated homes, to our respective privacies—in a word, back to our town.

No. We would not leave. We would stay.

We put on sweatshirts, heated up hot cocoa, and gathered by the fire. Those of us who employed more strategy watched the blizzard through our living room windows, watched it pile in heaps upon our lawns, imagining the possibilities when the thaw would come, when spring would emerge, when we would build again.

NORA'S SWEATSHIRT

Jim, Randy, and I had just started smoking pot. We barely knew how. At first, we used an apple, a technique Jim's older brother had shown us. Wherever we smoked—my house, Jim's house, or Randy's mom's apartment—we disposed of the apple pipe with the most careful attention to detail. For example, we didn't stuff it at the bottom of the garbage. Someone might smell it. We didn't chuck it outside into the neighbor's yard. Someone might find it, smell it, and turn it over to the police. Our fingerprints were on that apple. Instead, we'd chop the apple up and stuff it down the garbage disposal, or flush it down the toilet, or just eat it. These, we thought, were foolproof methods of disposal.

After we got the hang of it, we grew braver and restless. We drove around the rural countryside of Elm County, apple in tow, looking for our next great revelatory experience. I was the only one with a car, an old Chrysler Concorde my parents gave me, and I took us by the cows and cornfields, the farmhouses and soybean fields, the woody banks of our Missouri River oxbow. While driving, we liked to play homemade tape recordings of our attempt at a band. We'd nod our shaggy heads and say, "Sounds good, man" or "Badass," dreaming big, even though the sound quality was shit and the instruments sounded like hissy white noise.

We were fifteen. We were freshman. We fit together perfectly, Jim, Randy, and I. Jim was the big one, already over six feet and two hundred pounds. I was in the middle, three or four inches shorter and forty pounds lighter. Randy was no more than five-two. He actually had to gain weight to wrestle at one-hundred and three pounds.

Eventually we started smoking out of a Dr. Pepper can. It became our first regular pipe, the first thing we used more than once. Again, the methodology and technique were imparted to us by Jim's brother, a legendary pot smoker. He loved it so much he dropped out of college for it. Well, that and cocaine.

So Jim bent the pop can just so and poked little holes in the necessary places and I drove us out of Civil Bend and down South Dakota Highway 50. I went further than we'd ever gone, past the road where you could turn right and head towards the hills and be in Iowa in five minutes. I decided to be spontaneous and turned off the highway onto a paved county road I'd never taken.

The hills became steeper in these parts, more forested, the houses less frequent. Eventually we came upon a little country cemetery. I think Randy spotted it. He was always absent-mindedly noticing things. We pulled off the highway and parked safely out of view behind some trees.

A spiky black fence enclosed the old stone graves, which numbered exactly fourteen. It made me think of my brother Trent, who was one year older. When we were little, my mom dressed us alike, and sometimes people thought we were twins. We shared sports, action figures, had the same friends. It happened quickly and without a clearly identifiable cause, but by high school we had completed our growing-apart process. We didn't hang out, and we didn't share mutual friends. I didn't know him anymore. I only knew that, at sixteen, he drank all the time and—the reason the cemetery reminded me of him—was obsessed with death.

"Hey look at that tree," said Jim.

A lone, nondescript deciduous tree stood about ten yards from the cemetery gate, apart from the forested tree line, like a general in front of his cavalry. What really made it stand out was the rope hanging from one of its branches. We thought that rope was the coolest thing ever, and we tied it into a noose and smoked under the tree. That's what we took to calling it: the tree.

We dug a little hole and stuffed our pop can in there, covered it with twigs and leaves. A little careless, yes, but we were safely in the middle of nowhere, miles from anyone. At least that's what it seemed like when you looked up at the open sky or gazed into the wooded thicket. There were shadows, and all you felt was stillness.

Around this same time, Trent was getting on my nerves with his incessant mourning of people whom he knew, at best, casually. "Bryan's frickin' stepdad died today, man," he said one night at supper. "That's three people I know in the last two months who've died." Bryan was Trent's friend Bryan Utter, and Bryan's stepdad lived in Denver, some 650 miles southwest of our little town in the southeastern corner of South Dakota. I knew for a fact Trent had never met Bryan's stepdad.

"I bet you were really close to him," I teased.

"Dillon," my mom scolded, even though I'd had private conversations with her in which I expressed my belief that Trent had no right to be in mourning of people he barely knew, and she had conceded that she, too, found his constant verbal obituaries tiring. My mom turned to Trent and said, "The best thing you can do is just be there for Bryan."

"It's just so hard. Everybody close to me dies." He hung his head and dropped his fork on his plate, the metal clanking. He sobbed softly.

I shook my head and sighed. Loudly. On purpose. I looked to my dad for support, but he just continued to chew his food. He stayed out of stuff like this, delegated the mediating of brotherly disputes to my mom.

It was worse when Trent drank. He'd get sloshed every weekend and pretty tuned up most weeknights. It was strange, though, because he wouldn't slur his speech or stumble at all. He'd drink to this certain point at which his eyes glazed over, and then he'd just start bawling about all the people he knew who'd died. It was as if he'd already lived an entire lifetime—or several—and everyone he loved had perished long ago. I suspected it was all a ploy by Trent to get attention, but the truth was I didn't know where it came from, nor did I make an effort to learn.

He also started criticizing me for smoking pot. How did he find out? It was Civil Bend. Secrets were public knowledge. One night while my parents were out, we were drinking in the basement — Jim, Randy, and I. Trent came home around midnight, crashing our party. He hadn't quite reached that sobbing state of anguish. Instead, he was angry.

He said to me, "You're a fucking pothead."

I said, "So?"

"You're a worthless druggie." *Druggie* was the ultimate Elk Point drug pejorative, worse than stoner or burnout.

"You're a worthless alcoholic."

Trent came at me, fists flying. I absorbed a shot to the cheek, barely felt it. I wrapped my arms around him and brought him to the ground. He kicked and screamed. Randy and Jim just sat in their spots on the couch and recliner, respectively, amused and entertained.

I should mention that my parents adopted Trent when he was five days old from a seventeen-year-old girl from Sioux Falls. I came along a year after that, and, fifteen years later, had two inches and twenty pounds on him. I held him facedown on the floor until he agreed to give it up. I let him go and he dashed from the basement living room and up the stairs.

Randy and Jim shook their heads and chuckled. They'd seen Trent and me fight plenty of times, but it had never gotten physical. A minute later, Trent reappeared with a 20-gauge shotgun pointed at me. It was the one and only time I ever had a gun pointed at me.

I laughed.

Trent's eyes were red and moist and he cocked the gun and said, "Keep laughing, motherfucker."

"Come on, dude, put the gun down," Randy said.

I knew Trent would never shoot me. His finger wasn't even on the trigger.

Trent laid the gun against the wall and sat down. We apologized to each other. Everything cooled down. Trent got drunker and started whining about some friend of his from Beresford named Zach Hardy who had shot himself. I loved Zach Hardy so much and Zach Hardy was such a good friend of mine and on and on. Rather than sit and listen to that drivel, I suggested to Jim and Randy that we get an apple out of my parents' fridge.

We were at the tree, had just finished a few bowls off the can. We'd gotten used to the tree, the cemetery, our little spot, and we were ready for the next big thing to happen. Randy pointed north down the county road—the direction opposite Civil Bend—towards the top of a hill we couldn't see over. "Let's see what's up the road," he said.

We climbed in my car and ascended the hill, which led to more steeply rolling hills. As we headed north, the tree cover to our right grew thicker and thicker. "It's like a forest out here," I said.

"Whoa," said Randy, pointing out the window. A space had been cleared from the trees at the top of a hill and a log mansion stood large and proud like a castle, taller than the trees surrounding it.

Jim said "We could record our first album there" just as the tape recording skipped and cut out, then jumped to a spot several beats ahead.

A few miles later, we ascended the steepest hill yet, and, upon descending the crest, came on a strange ravine. To our right was the continuous forest and to our left, there were two houses and what looked like an Old West style general store.

"What the hell?" said Jim.

I turned down the music and when we reached the hill's base, just before passing the general store, a posted green sign said "Nora" and beneath that "Population 5." Time slowed to a crawl, or maybe I applied the brake, but it felt like we passed in front of that sign for ten minutes. I heard the words "Nora Population 5" in my brain like some kind of esoteric mystical chant, over and over, and I saw a vision of the sign in my head, even as I stared at it.

"Holy shit! Did you see that?" Randy said.

"Nora Population 5," I yelled.

"Turn around," Jim yelled.

There were no cars for miles and I flipped around and pulled up to the storefront. It was actually just a regular-looking, off-white two-story country house, except that it had a saloon awning over the front with the words "Nora General Store" painted in red letters.

I shut off my car, my heart pounding. I'd never heard anyone in town ever mention anything about Nora. Ever. I wasn't exactly lost, but I didn't know where we were, either—how many miles we were from Civil Bend, how far we were from the closest towns, Alcester, Beresford, and Akron.

"We're going in," Jim said, opening the passenger door and climbing out.

It was just Randy and I. I met his eyes in the rearview mirror. "We have to," he said, and got out. I checked myself in the mirror. Of the three of us, my eyes always got the reddest—double pinkeye, I called it—and this time was no different. I opened my door and followed Jim and Randy.

There was no open sign or store hours posted. Just a regular door atop a three-step concrete stoop. Jim knocked, and a few seconds later, it opened. We reeked like pot.

A plump, middle-aged man with greasy grey hair and a scraggly beard stood before us. His brown-rimmed bifocals were so thick they looked like Plexiglas. I don't know how he could see us through them. I immediately thought: this guy either repairs antique time-pieces or he has children locked in his basement.

"Hi there," he said, chuckling to himself. "Welcome to the Nora General Store."

We said hi in unison like triplets.

"What are your names?" he asked, looking directly into my eyes.

I swallowed before answering, my mouth drained of saliva. I desperately wanted cologne and Visine. And water. I said, "Dillon."

"Dillon what?"

I thought: make something up, make something up. "Dillon Wilcox," I said, as if reporting for duty. He went down the line: "Randy." "Randy what?" "Randy Ballinger." "Jim . . . Jim Cunningham."

"Come in," the man said, opening the door further and backing in. He had a gimp in his right leg, and his shoulder dipped with each step. "Let me show you around."

Inside, the place was enormously large and open, the ceiling almost two stories high. This is because the room housed, at its center, an old, beat-up wood-carved pipe organ. I'd never seen one up close. "Does it work?" I gasped.

Huge brass pipes stood on either side of the wood console like the columns of the Parthenon, rising all the way to the ceiling. At the console's center, three rows of keyboards elevated at staggered levels in a kind of keyboard staircase. A wood pedalboard of expression pedals ran along its base.

"Yeah it works," the man said. "Sometimes I have concerts here. I have them every Christmas."

"Can you play us something?" Jim asked.

"Sure."

He hobbled over to the organ and seated himself at the console. As he did, I took in the rest of the room. It was mostly bare except for a row of old chairs encircling the walls. At various spots hung tattered wreaths and Christmas stockings, and on one of the windowsills stood

three wood nutcrackers. The paint on them was chipped, and they
possessed the eerie veneer of forsaken porcelain dolls.

Suddenly, a deep burst of bass filled the room. My neck jerked
and my body stiffened to attention. The man held the chord for
several elongated moments, then ornamented it with a melodic
fluttering of shrill notes.

He removed his hands from the keyboard, and the room
went silent.

"Wow," Randy said.

"Okay, here goes."

He launched into "Angels We Have Heard on High," and the
room thickened with music. What I mean by that is you could
reach out and tangibly touch the notes in the air, as if the sounds
were sheets of gelatinous material circling about your hands, or
crawling on your neck, or vibrating down your spine.

The man—the organist—looked like the pilot of some strange,
medieval flying invention. His hands moved up and down the
stack of keyboards—pressing buttons, turning knobs and dials, it
seemed. His legs moved up and down, as if he were pedaling a
bicycle, and his feet moved back and forth along the pedalboard,
pushing down and releasing, down and releasing.

What's funny is I hate Christmas music—I always have—but I
closed my eyes and let the room fill with country people come on
a dark, frigid December night. Maybe they all drank hot chocolate
to keep warm, I don't know. And maybe there were marshmal-
lows in their mugs, melting together into a thick white foam. And
maybe they sang along together like they do in church, "Joy to
the World," "Silent Night," "O Little Town of Bethlehem," "We
Three Kings," and the works.

I breathed in Christmas carols, swallowing, forcing them down
my throat. But they'd disgorge in my chest, reverberating like a
drill, and work their way back up my palate and out my mouth in
exhale. I opened my eyes and thought: How rurally 19th Century
European it all seemed.

Of course, once he was done playing, we had to hound him with the story of our band.

"I play guitar," I said.

"I play bass," Randy said.

"I play drums," Jim said.

We told him how all our equipment was in Jim's parents' basement, how we played original, instrumental compositions which were totally in the vein of psychedelic post-punk art rock, how we recorded ourselves with a tape recorder and listened to it in my car, how we'd played at a few parties and were looking to book gigs in bars but we weren't old enough, how we were eventually going to move to Omaha and get a record deal with Saddle Creek Records. Like Bright Eyes. You've heard of Bright Eyes, haven't you?

Of course he hadn't. But he offered us milk and cookies, which gave him the connotative aura of Santa Claus. We sat in the chairs along the walls and ate our snacks and he told us about Nora.

"It's kind of strange, but I don't even know my neighbors. Those two houses you saw? I barely know the people who live there. There's an older couple in one of them, but they're not friendly. They keep to themselves. The other house is pretty much vacant. Some guy from Vermillion owns it, but he's never there."

"So it's pretty much just you and that couple," Randy said. "It's really Nora Population 3, not 5."

The man laughed. "Yeah, that's right. We're down to three."

He told us a little more about how he grew up in some little town I'd never heard of. They had a pipe organ in the church, though, and that's where he learned to play. He never married or had any kids, and he eventually reached a point where he didn't have to work anymore. So he moved to Nora and bought his own pipe organ.

A few chairs down from me, I spotted a purple Beresford Watchdogs sweatshirt. At a break in the conversation, I pointed at the sweatshirt and said, "Do you support the Watchdogs?"

The man looked confused for a moment, but his eyes followed

my finger and he said, "Oh that. Oh, no, that belonged to a boy who used to do some work for me. He, uh, he died not too long ago."

"Really?"

The man nodded, his face suddenly tight, solemn. "Yeah. He was a good kid. A really good kid. He'd come out here and sweep and clean and help with the chickens." He pointed with his thumb over his shoulder. "I've got some chickens out back."

I got up, fetched the sweatshirt, and sat back down. Staring at it, I said, "Was his name Zach? Zach Hardy?"

The man looked at me, his eyes wide. "Yeah. Did you know him?"

"No," I said. "But my brother did."

I clutched the sweatshirt tightly. The material felt different now that I knew who it used to belong to. I handed the sweatshirt to the organist. He took it. He rubbed it between his thumb and index finger. "He was a good kid," he repeated.

I didn't think, I just asked, "Why did he do it?"

The man shook his head. "I don't know," he said, his eyes on the sweatshirt. "He did a lot of drugs." He looked up at us. "Hard drugs. He wasn't happy. But I thought he was doing better. I thought he'd turned a corner."

I stood up and said, "We have to go. I need to get home."

He thanked us for coming, told us to stop by again. But I walked out in the middle of his goodbye speech. I went to my car and started it, waited for Jim and Randy.

They got in a minute later, and Jim said, "What's wrong, man?"

"Do you guys even know who Zach Hardy is?"

"Yeah, he's that guy Trent knew from Beresford who shot himself," Randy said. "That's crazy he worked here at the Nora General Store." He laughed after that, probably because of the whole absurdity of the Nora General Store and the pipe organ and its organist, all of that, not because of Trent and his grieving.

But I got defensive. "That's Trent's *friend*," I said.

Jim turned the music up and I'm not sure if they even heard me.

"We should jam with that guy," Jim said.

"What was his name?" Randy asked as I pulled onto the highway.

"What *was* his name?" Jim said.

When I asked my mom about Nora, she said, "Oh sure. The Nora General Store. There's the guy with the pipe organ. I've been to a few of his Christmas concerts."

"Really?"

"It's been years."

"What's his name?"

She shook her head. She looked confused, like I'd asked her if she ran into John Lennon at work that day. She said, "I don't know his name."

"Where'd he come from?" I asked. "Like, when did he suddenly appear in Nora?"

"Years ago," my mom said. "But I'm not sure where he came from."

"Does anybody?"

She shrugged.

"Is he related to anyone in town?"

"I don't think so."

"Isn't it weird nobody knows anything about him?"

"It is weird," she said with encouragement.

That weekend, we were at a bonfire party out in the country, off a gravel road by some grain silos. We told everyone about Nora, but no one was interested. They'd nod and say, "That's cool" and walk away, back to the keg or to some other, less esoteric group of people. We made a pipe out of a beer can and smoked. It was a pretty typical night—Jim, Randy, and I standing around hoping to get laid but instead just getting high, talking about how no one else in this town knew anything about music.

Trent was there, and towards the end of the night, when the

gathering had all but thinned out, he was leaning against his car, talking to a girl two grades above him, a senior. And she was listening to him. Trent had the magic like that.

But not on this night. In a few minutes, the girl got in her car and drove off, and it was just Trent, standing by his car, orange in the glow of the nearby fire. We watched as he shifted his stance back and forth. He jerked his shoulders and grunted, as if he were trying to break free of a straitjacket. Then the sobs came.

We reached him as the tears fell. He covered his face and turned away from us.

I uncharacteristically put my hand on Trent's back and said, "What's wrong?"

"Fuck off," he said.

"Come on," Randy said. "Tell us what's wrong."

Trent uncovered his face and said, "What do you care?"

Instead of telling him why we cared, I said, "Have you ever heard of Nora?"

At first, he shook his head, wanting no part of it. But we told him where it was, described how to get there. He stood still, suddenly calmer. We described the ravine, the green sign for Nora, the saloon awning, and the general store. His ears perked up, and he leaned forward a little, bending towards our voices. That's the thing about Trent. He listened. He even listened to our band, and no one cared about our band.

We told him about the pipe organ and the mysterious organist. We gesticulated wildly as we told him how the Christmas music filled the room. Meanwhile, the party thinned out, the bonfire dimmed.

We got to the last part, the part about Zach Hardy. I said, "I found Zach Hardy's sweatshirt in Nora. The guy said that Zach worked there."

"Really?"

Trent's eyes were dry now. Everyone had gone home. It was just the four of us standing by Trent's car. We watched the fire burn and slowly die, like the fading of an organ chord, and we listened, at least I did, to Trent talk about what Zach Hardy was like. And it didn't matter how well Trent knew him. Or if he knew him at all.

OLIVER WESTON GBV

I WORRY *BEE THOUSAND* is too stereotypical of a vinyl album for an Austin record party. I worry there will be an Ultra-Austinite there, and he or she will say, "Oh, how cute. He's still going through his '90s Guided By Voices phase"—as if they're a band that you're supposed to have digested entirely by a certain stage in life. And then the whole party will turn against me, swayed by the influence of the Ultra-Austinite with the encyclopedic knowledge of indie rock, *Britannica* and *World Book* combined. And then, even worse, the big scene in my TV show would be ruined, which is basically my life's work, which I can't stand when other people don't take seriously. But I think *Bee Thousand* could be that special record that strikes the balance of obscurity and good lo-fi that sends Austinites into the convulsive head bobbing associated with ecstasy overdose and the celebratory confirmation of terminal uniqueness relative to the rest of America. What I'm trying to say is, I didn't choose this record. Guided By Voices chose me thirty-seven weeks ago, and I've been following it ever since.

I pull the record from the row and stare at the guy with the purple cone-shaped wizard cap and purple, star-dotted cape on the cover. I look exactly like him. A spitting image. I already own thirty-seven copies of this record. This will be my thirty-eighth.

Every Tuesday I come to Hi, How Are You Records, and

each week there are flyers for the hottest Bring Your Own Record Record Party in all of Austin, and each week I buy another copy of *Bee Thousand*. But the last thirty-seven times, I haven't gone to the party. Instead, I've just sat in my little apartment and listened to the record front to back, for its thirty-six minute and thirty-five second duration. Then I put the record back in the sleeve and stuff it next to its twin sisters and brothers and clones.

Look, I don't dress like the *Bee Thousand* wizard solely because I want to draw attention to myself. I do it because I'm the center-piece of a reality television show about myself. The scene involves me buying the record, which I've done, as I've said, on a weekly basis. Then I'm supposed to go to the party. At the party, the record is either a big hit or a big flop. I don't know which. They haven't told me yet. All I know is that *Bee Thousand* is the record I'm supposed to take.

I know what to do next because I receive interpretive signals, little symbolic gestures that appear in my immediate reality to guide me. With *Bee Thousand*, it's that the album starts playing over the store's speakers. I sing the words to "Hardcore UFO's." People point at me and laugh, slap their knees and backs. But before you know it, they're bobbing their heads and clapping. Afterward, I'm signing copies of the record. Donning the wizard costume was the next logical step. And when I sign albums, I don't sign my real name, which is Oliver Weston. Instead I sign "Wizard." I didn't choose the name. Some cute girl who wears au naturel deodor-ant which doesn't actually deodorize and who has a chain dangling from her nostril and tattoos on her neck and arms chose it for me. I'm certain she's my chosen love interest for the show.

The cue is a little late this time. I'm already making my way to the checkout at the front of the store before "Hardcore UFO's" starts playing.

Finally.

I sing and people gather around and there's the pleasantly stinky cute girl and she points at me and I can hear her say to her friends, "See? I told you he was real."

I sign sixteen copies of the record. It must be climbing the Billboard charts by now. I take a flyer for this week's Bring Your Own Record Record Party and look around for the girl. She's been lingering lately, and I get the sense that she wants to talk to me—another clue. I spot her just as she leaves with her friends. She smiles and waves at me.

The cameras for the show in Hi, How Are You Records are in the rows of records, the tour posters, and the glasses of the store clerk, Roger. He is a chubby burnout with wavy silver hair who claims to have played guitar one night for Jethro Tull when they came through town thirty-some years ago. He gives me a high-five before I leave.

Full disclosure: I'd like to go to the Bring Your Own Record Record Party with the tattoo girl, for my TV show or not.

God, it's so nice to be alone and at peace sometimes. Such a relief to be out of the limelight. Work does this for me. I get to just stand here at the counter and not have to perform or entertain. Don't get me wrong, I enjoy being famous for all the reasons ordinary people think they want to be famous, such as the transformation from otherwise invisible to suddenly desirable (i.e. me in the eyes of the tattoo girl). But it does get tiring. Like when I'm in line to get a sandwich or a Twinkie and the cameras are rolling and everyone's acting like they're not on TV and like they don't recognize me from the show. It's part of the whole realistic authenticity thing, the whole "I wasn't in on it" aesthetic. But inevitably, because my fame is too palpably manifest in their presence, someone breaks the fourth wall. It happens most often when I wear the wizard costume. Sometimes, though, it happens when I'm in normal getup. For instance, right now.

I'm standing at the counter of the store, and this guy walks in. He's a big time Ultra, sporting a magnificent slicked-back combover, a beat-up old tank top with the logo of an auto body repair shop that closed over twenty-six years ago, jeans tight as yoga pants, and wing tipped leather boots.

He demands to see the green Samsung Galaxy S5 that we bought off a girl yesterday. I ask him how he knows we got a green Samsung Galaxy S5 and he says because his ex sold it to us.

You see, we're sort of a racket. We bill ourselves as a cell phone repair shop, but what we really do is buy old phones from cell phone stores or from customers in off the street. But the thing is, the phones we buy have all the data from the previous owner still on them—all the text messages, all the pictures, the videos, internet history, all of it. Then we jack up the price and sell them to our clientele, who are mostly criminals, perverts, stalkers, or, like this Ultra, jealous-angry exes.

"Let me see that phone," the Ultra says. "I know you have it."

I had the previous day off, so I wasn't aware of any recently purchased S5. But I quick check the inventory and sure enough, there it is. I pull it out and hold it up.

"That's it," he says, snatching it out of my hand. As he does, I catch a whiff of his acrid au naturel scent, which, frankly, isn't near as pleasurable as the tattoo girl's.

He swiftly taps his thumb over the screen. "I knew it was you!" he yells and holds up the phone to me. On the screen is a picture of me in my wizard suit in Hi, How Are You Records. He slams the phone down on the counter. He points an emphatic index finger at me, his eyes a murderous rage, and says, "You're dead."

Then he storms out. I will admit, he looks damn slick ambling in his wingtips, kicking at the air in the parking lot on the way to his car.

I pick up the phone and scroll through more pictures of myself in the wizard suit. There are several. Several hundred. Mostly it's me singing between the rows of records, holding an imaginary mic to my mouth and gesticulating to the audience. Of course, the onlookers are enthralled. What can I say? I'm a showman.

But when I get to the selfies of the previous owner I nearly drop the phone. There is the cute, tattooed, pleasantly odorous girl! In the picture, the camera is elevated above her and she gazes upward, her oily chestnut hair swooping over one eye. In another picture, she has the camera held so far out you can see down her pasty white forearm to her bicep and up to her bushy armpit hair. My skin tingles. I have never seen anything so beautiful in my life. In another, again from above, I'm offered a liberal view of her cleavage, and at that point, I actually do drop the phone.

You see what I mean now about the interpretive signs and borderline cosmic nudges?

I know now that she's the chosen love interest. There's no other conclusion to arrive at. Still, there's the problem of the crazy Ultra ex and then there's the task at hand, which is digging through the green Samsung Galaxy S5 and learning everything there is to know about the tattooed girl.

"Mom, is it weird to know everything there is to know about a girl on your first date?" I ask.

"You mean like before you've even met her?"

"Yeah."

My mom's face scrunches together. "Yes, Olly. It's weird and creepy."

Once a week, my mom cooks me dinner at her place. Technically, I have a dad. But I have no idea who he is. Neither does she, really. He took off before my first birthday, never to be seen again. No goodbye or anything. Just gone. I grew up wondering who my dad was. I started worrying he could be anybody, any man on the street. I imagined him watching me, lurking in the shadows spying, following me. I still think this sometimes when I'm not thinking about the TV show. In fact, before the tattoo girl, I either thought about my current TV show or whether or not my dad was watching me. And sometimes cell phones, but only at work.

"Her name's Tess," I say, and begin regurgitating everything I learned from investigating the tattoo girl's phone. "She's my age, twenty-five. She's from Massachusetts. She moved here, from what I've gathered, right after high school. She works at Yankee Hotel Foxtrot Diner, that vegan place on Handley Avenue. From the pictures and videos I've seen, she performs some light animal activism—corner-protest-homemade-sign-holding, pamphlet-handing-outing—that sort of thing. Nothing crazy. From her listening history, it's evident she likes punk, hip-hop, house, and especially Lauryn Hill. Holy crap does she like *The Miseducation of Lauryn Hill*."

My mom looks concerned, like I just said something crazy. "Did you learn all that on her Facebook page?"

"Um, yeah," I lie. She doesn't know about the true nature of my job. She thinks we just repair cell phones.

"I think you ought to hold back on how much you let on that you know about her," my mom says. "You don't want to sound like a stalker. Trust me, I went on a date with this one guy and he was really charming up until he started asking me about what it was like to grow up in Hamlin. But I hadn't mentioned that I grew up in Hamlin and then I started thinking back about other things leading up to that question. For example, his wearing a red shirt and red shoes and red being my favorite color. His insistence on mentioning how much he loved *Friends*, which happens to be my favorite TV show. His suggesting that we go to Raziel's, my favorite restaurant, and then his ordering for me, without having to ask, the mostaccioli santioni, my favorite dish. I got up and walked out, Olly. You don't want to be that guy."

"But mom, it's the next step in my, um," I stumble, choosing my words carefully, but her eyes light up. She's already on to me. "It's the next thing for my *project*."

She frowns. "Olly, are you back to thinking you're on TV again?"

That's the only thing about my mom. She's forty-two and she's still beautiful and she's sweet and kind and pays my rent every now and then, but she got me "help" when she thought I needed it, which meant a psych ward and therapists. I neither wanted nor needed that kind of help, but I understand it was out of love that she did it because that's what she told me and she's never lied to me.

But she refused to believe me about my last two TV shows. I'll admit, they weren't very popular. They aired on YouTube. And I'm going to step aside here for a second and say that the comments on my first two shows really pissed me off. It's like no one *got it*, you know? They're like, "Who's this crazy guy wearing a baggy green Adidas sweatsuit from the '80s breakdancing on a sheet of cardboard on the street corner?" And I'll be honest, I'm not sure who recorded me and posted the videos, but that's not the point. The point is. I mean the point was. Well, I forget what the point was, but it was important. It was *real*, you know?

"Olly, look at me. Are you doing the TV show thing again?"

I swallow. "No," I say, shaking my head.

"Olly. Are you telling me the truth?"

I nod. "Yeah. Of course. Look, I'm going on a date with this girl."

My mom's eyes widen. "You are?"

"Yeah, well, I mean yeah, I am. I just have to ask her. I'm going to ask her this Tuesday at Hi, How Are You Records. We're going to go to a Bring Your Own Record Record Party."

"Oh, Olly, you're still going to that record store?"

"Yeah but there's this girl there. Tess. Remember? I was just telling you about her."

My mom nods. She looks sad. "I just wish you wouldn't go to that record store and sing."

"Why not?"

"It's just, well, it's just that they *laugh* at you, honey."

"Yeah, because they're having fun. Because I entertain them. Look, mom, I don't expect you to understand. It's all part of the sh—" I stop myself. "It's all to get this girl to like me."

My mom nods. She won't stop staring at me. She won't blink, and I hate it when she won't blink.

"Olly, I'm serious. If you're doing the TV thing again, I'm getting you help."

"Jesus Christ, I'm not doing the god damn fucking TV thing,"

I yell, not meaning to. I pound the tabletop, not meaning to do that either. Sometimes it just happens when people don't believe me. I can't exactly control it.

My mom shudders. I see worry on her face and terror in her eyes. But she breathes and regains composure.

"Look at me. Look at me, Olly. There's no TV show."

I nod. Her eyes are moist.

"I want to hear you say it."

"There's no TV show," I say, looking directly into the camera, which is hidden in the door of the fridge behind my mom.

That last part was a bit of acting. Of course there's a TV show. I mean, her ex wants to kill me. That's a TV plot if I've ever heard one.

The next Tuesday, I'm back in Hi, How Are You Records, dressed as the wizard, holding *Bee Thousand*, waiting for my cue. Everyone's here, including Tess. She's wearing a short black-and-white polka dot skirt and a stitched-together shirt that says "Go Vegan." But I'm thinking it ought to say "Go Oliver Weston."

Her Ultra ex is lurking in the corner. He thinks I don't recognize him because he's grown a beard and wears *Miami Vice* sunglasses, but I'd know that oily comb-over anywhere, and his holey old T-shirt commemorating a rural county tractor pull from 1977, which he obviously isn't old enough to actually have competed in, is a dead giveaway.

Roger hits the button and "Hardcore UFO's" plays and I do what I do best. It's a particularly successful performance (or should I say episode?), and I feel like this time, the thirty-ninth, is the charm. I sign twenty-two copies of the record and snatch a copy of *The Miseducation of Lauryn Hill* and quick pay Roger for it and my thirty-ninth copy of *Bee Thousand*.

"Tess!" I say, catching up to her on her way out the door.

We're standing face to face on the sidewalk, under the store's awning. The Austin traffic is jammed bumper to bumper—our live audience.

"How did you know my name?" Tess asks. But she doesn't look mad. She looks flattered. So I go with it.

"I asked around," I say, and hand her *The Miseducation*. "Here, I got this for you."

"Oh my God," she says, joy spreading over her face. "This is my favorite record! I already have like four copies of it."

I hold up *Bee Thousand*. "This is my thirty-ninth copy of this record."

She laughs. Hard. But she's looking at me fondly. "I absolutely adore your performances in there. I love the wizard suit."

Perfect. So I say, "Will you go to the Bring Your Own Record Record Party with me? You can bring the record I just got you."

She laughs again. Her cheeks are red. But her eyes are telling. They're wide and studying, moistening, pulling at me. She smiles just as I catch a whiff of her musty scent, and I smile back.

She says, "I've been waiting for you to ask me to go to the Record Party for about as long as you've been buying that record."

Whoa. Some pretty sentimental scriptwriting, that, but I'll admit it feels amazing.

She takes my arm and says, "Come on, my wizard. Take me to get a soy latte and vegan cupcakes."

I let her lead me down the sidewalk, and for several moments, I forget about the cameras entirely because I keep stealing glances at Tess now that she's up close. And I realize I love everything about her. Her hugely gauged earlobes. Her sword and shield and talon tattoos creeping up her neck. Her stenciled eyebrows. Her wing-like eyelashes. Her love of Lauryn Hill and her love of my wizard costume and her searching eyeballs and scraggly armpit hair and distinct olfactory essence.

But I'm slapped back to reality as we arrive at the coffee shop when, just before entering, I glance back and see the Ultra ex trailing a block behind us.

"Maybe I should take off the wizard suit," I say.

"No, leave it on," Tess says and pulls me into the store and drags me up to the counter.

Outside, the ex stands with his back to the store window. Intermittently, he glances over his shoulder, lowers his shades for a moment. I've never done any physical confrontation on camera, but that seems like the direction this is all going.

Over soy lattes (yuck) and vegan cupcakes (pretty good, actually), I do the exact opposite my mom recommended and information dump everything I know about Massachusetts, which consists mostly of Revolutionary War factoids about Boston, such as that tea was dumped in protest of the Crown because, you know, tea is an important British national symbol. Also, Harvard is there. Not in Boston, but some small city right outside of it.

"Cambridge," Tess says. "I'm not actually from Boston. I'm from Worcester. It's in Western Massachusetts."

Then I tell her everything I know about animals, which is that they have anatomies and live in ecosystems and survive by eating each other or hiding from each other, depending on whether they're a predator or prey. Although some eat plants.

I sound like an idiot and she laughs and her cheeks are red. I say "Circuses are bad and exploitative and abusive" and she laughs even more and says, "God, you are the cutest thing ever. Let's go to the Party." She grabs my hand and leads me out the door and I'll admit, I could get used to her holding my hand and taking me places.

We take a cab to Rosedale, where there's the highest concentration of Ultras in all of Austin. We get dropped off at a place called Funky Monkey. It's a dilapidated coffee shop/bar. When I climb out of the car, of course I spot Tess's ex lurking around the corner.

His head is poking out past the corner of a brick wall. When he sees me, his head disappears.

At the door of Funky Monkey, we hand our records to the bouncer, a scrawny hippie with dreadlocks, and he inspects them. If they're not up-to-Ultra-standards, we can get turned away. I know *The Miseducation* is a go, but I worry slightly about *Bee Thousand*. The bouncer looks at the album's cover and then looks at me in my wizard suit. "Oh, ha. I get it," he says, handing me my record. "Go on in."

Inside, I gasp. I've never seen so many Ultras in one place in my entire life. And I've lived my entire life in Austin. The place is crawling with them. Guys with black-rimmed glasses and shaved sides and oily comb-overs and skinny jeans and tank-tops and esoteric tattoos and well-groomed bushy beards. They all look like Tess's ex. How am I going to be able to tell which is him? The girls wear anachronistic hodgepodge thriftware outfits, army boots, cowboy boots, boots that look like shoes but are boots, their hair matted and uncombed. Oh, and the *smell*. When it's just Tess, I don't mind it, in fact I like it. But it's like Tess times however many people are here. Probably fifty. So you can imagine.

We place our records in the record bin where they will be selected at random by DJ whatever. No, that's actually his name, DJ whatever.

ABBA's "Dancing Queen" comes on and Tess grabs both my hands and says, "Oh my god I love this song! It's so kitsch." She pulls me onto the dance floor and for the next hour I get to do things with a girl I've never done before, such as put my hands on Tess's hips and around her shoulders. She smooches me on the cheek in between each song the way my mom used to when I was little. And she whispers things in my ear like "You're a great dancer," which I already knew, being a performer and all, and "You're so handsome," which I had never been told. She also says "I really like you" and an intense fizzling rises in my chest and I get goosebumps and I say "I really like you, too."

And all this time I completely forget about the cameras. I don't care where they are, what they're seeing, whether they have good angles on us or not. I just love looking into Tess's eyes and having her look back into mine and pull me close and then pull away, over and over again. Right in the middle of The Cure's "It's Friday, I'm in Love" Tess yanks me to her—even though it's Tuesday—and presses her lips against mine. She opens her mouth. I open mine and let her tongue in and touch mine to hers and we swirl them around together. I realize our tongues are dancing and I pull my head away and say, "Our tongues are dancing." She giggles and presses against the back of my head, pushing my face back to hers, and continues kissing me.

"Hardcore UFO's" starts playing and Tess goes nuts, jumping up and down, pointing at me and telling me to do my thing. So I do it. The whole place stops dead in its tracks and forms a circle around me. Someone hands me a mic and I sing and dance. It's easily the greatest performance of my life. I go all-out theatrical, pretending I'm flying like a real wizard, holding my arms to the heavens as if lightning bolts are shooting out of my hands.

The Ultras eat it up, showering praise on me once the song is finished. Tess comes back to my side and I put my arm around her, comfortably, naturally. But there's one disgruntled Ultra.

Tess's ex comes up to us, removes his shades and slams them on the ground. They snap in half. It's time for the showdown.

"Listen, buddy," he says (scriptwriting cliché), "That's my girl-friend you're with."

He removes his cardigan, revealing the 1977 tractor pull T-shirt.

I point and say, "You did not compete in that tractor pull competition."

"No shit. My dad did. Let's go, Wizard."

He puts up his fists.

"Let it go, Victor," Tess says. "Leave us alone." Then Tess turns to me. "He's my crazy ex. I dumped him like three months ago and he won't leave me alone. Don't fight him. Let's just walk away."

She leads me for a few steps when Victor says, "He snooped through your phone, Tess! He works at that cell phone place!"

Tess turns around says, "No shit. I *wanted* him to snoop through it. That's why I took it there."

"Whoa, whoa, whoa," I interject. "Tess, I only snooped through your phone for the TV show. That was how they told me you were the love interest, and that's why I snooped through it. That's all. I wasn't being nosy. I was just doing what they wanted."

"What are you talking about?" Tess says, her face scrunching up like my mom's. "TV show?"

I glance around at the crowd of Ultras. They're all watching. The place is silent. The lights are turned up. I say, "The reality show about me."

"What?" Tess laughs, her cheeks reddening. "What reality show? Where are the cameras?"

"There." I point at one of the large speakers. "And there." I point at a strobe light. "And there and there." I point at a female Ultra and the bin of records.

The smile leaves Tess's face. She takes a step closer to me and says, very softly, "Do you think your life is a TV show?"

To which Victor bellows in laughter and points at me and says, "He's a lunatic! He thinks there's cameras filming his life!"

"Do you not believe me?" I ask.

Victor cackles on and says, "He's batshit crazy!"

"Say it again," I yell, not meaning to raise my voice. I push my way past Tess. "Say it again to my face."

"The wizard is bat-shit-fucking crazy!"

Remember when I said I do things I don't mean to do when people don't believe me? Well, I charge at this Victor guy and knock him down and I'm on top of him pummeling his face with my fists and I know I feel Tess behind me, pulling at my arms and shoulders, saying "Don't! Don't!" But I keep going and going and to be honest, I don't clearly remember what happened after that, only that I could hear the sound of sirens and Tess crying and my mom's voice saying "TV show" and "for years" and "help."

When I awake, it takes several aggressive blinks to clear the fog. I see my mom. She's sitting at my bedside. She looks drained, like she's experienced prolonged heightened anxiety. When she sees my eyes are open, she takes my hand.

"Olly."

"What happened?" I say.

My mom sighs and chuckles at the same time. A doctor comes into view. He's well-put together, about the same age as my mom.

"What happened?" I repeat. I meet eyes with the doctor and ask, "Are you my dad?" I'm not saying it's likely, I'm just saying it's possible because, you have to admit, it would be a pretty amazing twist-ending to a TV show.

My mom laughs, not happily, more like resignedly, and shakes her head. The doctor glances uncomfortably at my mom, then turns to me. "You laid quite the beating on the other young man," he says. "He's actually a few rooms down."

Victor—the Ultra-Austinite ex from Hell.

"Don't worry," the doctor continues. "He'll be okay. But you did break his jaw. It took several people to restrain you. They had to administer a sedative."

I proudly hold up a clenched fist. "He didn't believe me about the TV show, doc."

"Olly, please," my mom says.

"What?" I say. It's fairly obvious. The cameras are in the television attached to the ceiling, the vital sign display device, and in the doctor's stethoscope. This is conspicuously building up to a season finale.

"There's a specialist coming to talk to you about the TV show," the doctor says.

"The producers? It's about time."

"No. Not the producers. A . . . uh, someone to help you with the show."

I hate that word help.

"You should also know that the other young man may very well press charges," the doctor says. "In which case, you'll have to talk to the police."

Now that's good drama. Getting law enforcement involved always cranks up the tension.

The doctor leaves. My mom stares at me without blinking. Moisture fills her eyes and she puts her hands over her face.

"Mom, it's okay." I reach for her hand. She takes it and says, "No, it's not. It's not okay, Olly. It's not okay. I want you to get better."

I squeeze my mom's hand and suddenly remember holding Tess's hand. My chest fizzles the way it did on the dance floor and, talk about a perfect ending, Tess appears in the doorway and walks up to the bed.

"You're awake," she says.

My mom looks up and sniffles. "I got to meet your friend Tess while you were out cold."

"Tess has great taste in music," I say. I look at Tess. "She loves Lauryn Hill."

Tess laughs, but her eyes get moist, too.

"It's true," she says.

She comes to the side of the bed and takes my other hand. I feel warm and robust with my mom and Tess holding my hands, like I could rise from this bed and take them out to dinner at the best vegan restaurant in all of Austin, which is really saying something because this is Austin.

"Maybe they'll shoot a second season," I say to Tess. "Like a follow-up episode, you know?"

She squeezes my hand. Her energy shoots up my arm and into my chest. I breathe her scent and feel it run through my body. Everything right now is so perfect.

"We'll work on the TV thing," Tess says, which I know means she doesn't believe me, but I don't care. When she holds my hand and looks at me the way she does, the cameras don't matter. The fame, the fans, I'd give it up for her.

OF SMALL ACCOUNT

I TOLD HER NOT to, but Heidi 3-D printed a little boy. He came out thin with oily blonde hair and a dirty face. He looked to be maybe five or six, and he wanted nothing but to have a father. In fact, he wouldn't stop crying until he got one.

"You see? I knew this wasn't a good idea," I said.

I mostly meant that we couldn't afford to have a kid, not if we hoped to pay off the house. After all, Heidi and I worked at Soy-In-And-Out, a bottom-rung meatless fast-food joint.

Heidi said, "I can fix this."

She 3-D printed the boy a really good father. This guy was tall and handsome and slicked his hair back and wore an English-cut tailored suit. He had a big house in a nice neighborhood. Sure, this father worked a lot, but he came home every night, unlike some fathers. At any rate, he could afford to pay for the boy's college.

"I don't want this daddy!" the boy yelled. "I want *this* daddy!"

The boy latched onto my leg. I looked at Heidi. She was smiling. She walked up to us, and we group-hugged.

In this way, we became a family.

We named the boy Adam, after the first who was also, in a way, 3-D printed.

The day before Adam's first day of kindergarten, we took him to the store to buy clothes and school supplies. Heidi pushed the plastic cart, and Adam and I walked along either side of her. If you didn't know any better, you'd think Heidi and I 3-D printed our little Adam the old-fashioned way, if you know what I mean.

"My God," said Heidi, examining a spiral notebook, "they want *three dollars* for one of these?"

I showed her the school supply list from our local paper.

"It says we're supposed to get him *three* notebooks," I said.

"This stuff is all so expensive," Heidi said, glancing at the pencils, the scissors, and the folders.

I grabbed one of the cheap, ten-cent folders and put it in the car.

"I want *this* folder!" Adam said.

He held up the most expensive one there was, a shiny, Optimus Prime folder that cost sixty cents.

I wasn't all that serious, but I kind of was, when I said to Heidi, "You know, we can just 3-D print all this stuff."

"That's a *great* idea."

We abandoned the cart on the spot, which only contained off-brand glue, off-brand crayons, and the generic folder. Adam threw a fit, bemoaning our denial of Optimus Prime.

"It's not fair!" he screamed.

Heidi and I glanced around at the parental onlookers, judging us cruel and unfit parents, no doubt. Certainly the other children present felt fortunate not to have to go home with us, empty-handed as Adam was.

He started bawling.

I grabbed his hand and dragged him out of the store. I remember thinking in that moment that for a 3-D printed kid, Adam was a lot like all the other greedy, non-3-D-printed kids I'd ever known.

When we got home, we 3-D printed Adam all his clothes and

school supplies, including a passably semblant knockoff of the Optimus Prime folder. When we tucked him into bed that night, Adam was satisfied and eager to start school.

Again, I wasn't all that serious, but I kind of was, thinking about money and all, when I said in bed later that night, "You know, school is *so* expensive."

"I *know*," Heidi said. "Just think about all the lunch money he's going to need."

"That and stuff like band."

"And sports."

"Are you thinking what I'm thinking?"

Heidi and I jumped out of bed and dashed down to the 3-D printer, which we kept locked in a basement room, hidden from Adam. We hauled it out to the backyard and spent the rest of the night 3-D printing a small building, which would serve as his elementary school. We 3-D printed teachers, other six-year-olds, textbooks, even a pudgy bully with a too-tight striped shirt and a cowlick.

The next morning, after Adam had his breakfast, we waved goodbye to him. He walked out the backdoor, across the backyard, and into the little 3-D printed school, which we named Washington Elementary—the least suspicious-sounding name we could think of.

Heidi and I held each other in the kitchen and pretended like it was real, like we were watching our real son attend his first real day of school.

"We're *such* good parents," Heidi said.

I pulled her tight and kissed her, but only briefly. We had on our Soy-In-And-Out black slacks and polo shirts, and we had to be to work in fifteen minutes.

Over the next few years, we 3-D printed Adam new first, second, and third grade teachers: Mrs. Dobbs, Mr. Levinson, and Miss

Topf, respectively. When he joined the 3-D-printed little league baseball team in 4th grade, we 3-D printed all his opponents using substandard materials so that Adam would always win.

We really wanted to get Adam some real stuff—a real trumpet, say, or a real wooden bat, or a real human friend—but each month, when the mortgage payment came due, it was easier to just keep on 3-D printing our son all his needs. Plus, Heidi got promoted to Manager at Soy-In-And-Out, which meant that, in addition to getting to wear the gold Manager pport jacket over her black polo, she also got a raise. We started setting money aside for retirement. If you didn't know any better, which no one did because we didn't have any friends, you'd have thought we were actually successful.

In 5th grade, when Adam became interested in Eves, we 3-D printed him one of those, too.

The first Eve had auburn hair and freckles. She looked like the mascot of a long-defunct meat-centric fast food chain. Overall, I'd say she was a success. She gave our Adam his first hand-holding experience, which took place one day at the lunch table. We made her ask him to the 3-D printed school dance we held that fall, and we made Adam say yes. To this end, she provided Adam his first slow-dance experience, during which Heidi, as the parental chaperone, made sure Adam's hands stayed on Eve's hips and Eve's hands stayed on Adam's shoulders.

That summer, as he became more serious about baseball (he was a good shortstop), Adam broke up with the first Eve. He told her, "I just really need to focus on fielding grounders right now."

But by the next fall, he seemed ready, or at least Heidi and I were ready, for another Eve. To save a bit of money, we recycled some parts of the old Eve, and, this time, 3-D printed a tall brunette one. She was athletic and played softball. We figured shared interest might keep Adam from getting bored as quickly.

For a while, it worked. Adam and the brunette Eve played catch together, practiced hitting and pitching. But Adam didn't show any interest in Eve beyond having her as a glorified teammate.

Heidi and I spied on them often, and Adam didn't want to flirt with her or hold her hand, despite his other 3-D printed classmates all having boyfriends and girlfriends by that point.

We cornered Eve one night in the backyard while Adam was in his room studying.

"You know the All-School 3-D-Printed Dance is coming up," Heidi told her.

"Yeah," Eve said. "So?"

"So, are you going to ask Adam?"

"Um, probably not," Eve said. "I don't think he'd say yes."

"Why not?" I asked. "He seems to have taken a special liking to you."

Eve shook her head. "I don't think he likes, um, my kind. Not like that."

"What do you mean?"

"*Girls.* I don't think he likes girls."

"Really?" Heidi said.

"Yeah," Eve said. "He's always staring at Josh. You know Josh, the catcher on the team?"

It all became clear to me then.

"We don't need an Eve," I said to Heidi. "What we need is a *Steve.*"

So, using some of the spare parts of the brunette Eve, we 3-D printed a Steve. We tried our best to make him look vaguely like Josh, who was short and stocky with curly black hair. Sure enough, the second Eve had been right. Adam took an immediate liking to the mysterious new student who showed up the next day at school. Before long, Adam and Steve were spending every waking moment they could together.

Steve would meet Adam at our backdoor and they'd walk the ten paces to school together. By this time, we'd upgraded the elementary school into a junior high—Lincoln Junior High, to be exact—and Adam and Steve would linger between classes at each other's lockers, batting their eyes and flirtatiously running their hands along each other's chests and shoulders.

Through our constant spying and questioning of 3-D printed Lincoln Junior High students, we soon learned Adam and Steve were an exclusive couple. This made it a bit complicated when, one Thursday night at dinner, Adam asked if Steve, whom he referred to as his "best friend," could stay the night tomorrow.

Like any parents worth their salt, Heidi and I were committed to at once fostering the natural sexual growth of our child while also artificially prolonging his first real sexual encounter.

"How good of friends are you and Steve?" I asked.

"I told you. We're *best* friends."

"I think what your dad means to say is, are you and Steve friends with benefits?"

"Friends with benefits?" Adam said.

Heidi nodded. "Yeah. Like, you know, *benefits*."

Adam looked confused. "We learned about fringe benefits in social studies," he said.

"No," I said. "We're not talking about fringe benefits. Although those are good to have, and Soy-In-And-Out's could be better. We're talking about *sexual* benefits."

Adam's face turned red. He was a smart kid, and he could tell that we knew.

"So you know," he said.

Heidi smiled warmly and took hold of Adam's hand.

"Of course we know," she said. "Which is why Steve is welcome to stay, but he has to sleep on the couch in the living room."

Adam smiled, and the redness slowly left his face.

"Thanks, mom and dad."

I almost said something about unprotected sex leading to pregnancy, but fortunately stopped myself before opening my mouth. *Duh*, you know?

It all came crashing down because of a stupid oversight on our part: Sex Ed. Heidi and I hadn't even bothered to examine the contents of the Lincoln Junior High curriculum. We just 3-D printed it.

So one day at school, Mr. Jeffrey, the Sex Ed teacher who relayed the events of that day to us later on, taught Adam and his 7th grade classmates all about the process of human reproduction. This was kind of ironic since literally everybody at the school, including Mr. Jeffrey himself, had been 3-D printed and not sexually reproduced.

It became clear to the students something was off about the reproductive process Mr. Jeffrey spoke of, since none of them had actual parents who had had actual sex to produce them.

"Don't we come from a 3-D printer?" said Jessica Kemp.

"Yeah, that's what I always thought," said Benjamin Martinez.

"My earliest memories are of the insides of a machine that took raw materials and made them into limbs and a body and a face," said Darla Friedman.

"Technically, you're right," said Mr. Jeffery. "*We* come from a 3-D printer. But the School Board wanted you to learn how *humans* reproduce."

"Humans? Aren't we human?" said Steve.

Mr. Jeffrey shook his head. "No. We're 3-D objects."

"Who is the School Board?" asked Adam.

"You don't know?" Mr. Jeffrey said. "It's your parents, Guy and Heidi."

At that, Adam came storming all ten paces home, throwing open the backdoor. Heidi and I had gotten home from work shortly before and were preparing supper.

"Adam," Heidi said. "You're home early."

"Guess what we learned about in school today?" he said.

"What's that?"

"Human sexual reproduction."

"Shit," we both said, which gave it away. He knew.

"I want to know the truth," Adam said.

Heidi and I looked at each other, still in our Soy-In-And-Out garb. We had no choice. We led Adam down the basement stairs and into the room we kept locked.

I pointed at the 3-D printer. "That's where you come from."

Adam walked up to the 3-D printer and pressed the button. Out came a Steve. He pressed it again, and out came an Eve. He pressed the button again and again, until the room filled with Eves and Steves and friends and clothes and parts of schools.

"My whole life is a lie!" Adam screamed.

He looked at us accusingly. His eyes were moist, his face red.

I nodded.

I don't know what movie Heidi had recently seen, but she said, "Your life may be a lie, Adam, but our love for you is real."

This only made him angry.

"I hate you! Both of you!" Adam yelled. "I'm leaving and never coming back!"

He grabbed the hand of a nearby Steve—a husky one with olive skin—and together they darted out of the room.

We never saw our Adam again. Looking back, it's surprising Adam didn't figure out on his own he was 3-D printed. He was such a smart kid, but I guess even smart kids don't stop to wonder if they were 3-D printed rather than sexually reproduced.

But it's okay. We have a better setup now. Heidi and I ground up all the stuff from the old Adam's life and used it to 3-D print a new Adam. However, this new Adam never becomes truly self-aware because, before he does, he automatically removes his own rib and uses it to 3-D print a new Eve.

Then he dies, and the Eve grows and does the same thing with her rib. Then she dies, leaving us with an automated, low-main-tenance cycle of toddler Adams and Eves—which we learned the hard way are the best kind.

Now, we actually own our house outright as well as the Soy-In-And-Out franchise we work at, which is especially profitable nowadays.

If you didn't know any better, which no one does, you'd think our 3-D printed veggie burgers were actual veggie burgers, and that our 3-D printed employees actually got paid, which they don't, and that our whole 3-D printed life is an actual life, which it really isn't, but kind of *is*.

PUDDIN' SUITCASE

THE FAMILY GATHERED AT my Aunt Edna's for Mother's Day that year. We sat around the kitchen table. As usual, Edna and my mom asked if I was dating, said they knew of at least two young women in town in their mid-thirties who weren't married. But they knew, just like everyone did in a town as small as Civil Bend, that at least officially, I wasn't dating anyone. Unofficially, however, I'd begun to see Vince. He lived in Sioux Falls, about forty minutes north. He was a fitness instructor, and I liked that he took great care of himself. We'd been together almost six months. It was going well. So well, in fact, that as I sat before my family that day, I'd already decided that, after all these years, I was leaving my tiny hometown to live with Vince in the rural metropolis of Sioux Falls.

Some of the family knew. Edna's son Gerald knew. And my sister knew. But the matriarchs didn't, and I wasn't ready to tell them, though I felt they had their suspicions.

After our brunch of egg bake and fruit, our mothers opened their cards and, as is our tradition, read aloud the corny messages Hallmark had written them. When Edna opened hers, a picture fell out.

She swiped it off the table. "What's this?" she asked.

Gerald, wearing a big grin, said, "Mom, that's your new house."

Of course Edna recognized the modest, sky-blue one-story as the house Denny Jurgenson used to live in. That is, until Denny's kids moved him into the nursing home.

"Why would I want to move? I'm happy here," Edna said. "I'm not moving."

Her words were instinctual. Any seventy-three-year-old would say the same thing in response to their child showing up, having already used his money to snatch a part of her independence. Gerald, who lived five hours northeast in Minneapolis, had become a multi-millionaire in real estate. He covered whatever living expenses Edna's social security didn't and then some. When she began her decline, he gradually wrested more and more control from her, until he managed her life, at least it seemed to me, like a business venture.

"Now, mom, you fell down those stairs," Gerald said. He pointed towards the living room, towards the staircase, where she had fallen some months before and, thankfully, only bruised her forearm. "What's going to happen when you fall again? How bad is it going to be?"

To be sure, we all agreed that Edna ought to move into a smaller house. After her heart attack, she had slowed considerably. Her back and shoulders hunched. She walked with her hands clasped in front of her chest. Her stride shortened gradually into tiny baby steps. She had, however, managed to quit smoking for an entire year. But she picked that back up.

Edna's face tightened. Her cheeks flushed. She produced her Virginia Slims, stuck one in her mouth, and lit up.

"Aunt Edna, please," my sister said. "Not with the kids around."

"This is my house," Edna said.

My sister told the kids to go play outside, which they did. For the next several minutes, Edna and Gerald argued over whether or not Gerald could back out of the sale. Eventually, Gerald said, "That's it, mom. You can either move into Denny Jurgenson's old house or we can put you in the—

But he didn't have to finish. Edna cut him off. "All right, all right," she said. She picked up the picture of the blue house. "I suppose this can work."

After that, Edna calmed down, seemed to accept the situation. But she kept glancing out the window to the backyard. At first, I thought she was just watching the kids play. But she kept looking after they came back in.

When she got the far-away look in her eyes, it was so obvious I couldn't believe I'd missed it before. She was looking at the little plastic-flower wreath, half-destroyed over the years and leaning heavily to the side, that she'd staked over the spot where I had buried, five years before, her beloved poodle, Puddin'.

A week after Mother's Day, a For Sale sign went up in Edna's front yard. Gerald had called twice to request my services hauling boxes and furniture to Edna's garage, where she planned to have a little rummage sale before she moved. Then, a few days later, Edna called me herself at supper time.

"I need you to dig up Puddin'," she said. "I want him with me in my new yard."

Vince was over for supper. I'd made a tangy meatloaf with steamed potatoes. We were just sitting down to eat.

Though I'd heard her clearly, I said, "You want me to *what?*"

"Bobby, please," Edna said.

I glanced at the meatloaf on the dining table. Suddenly, it became the half-decomposed poodle: exposed patches of bone, rotting entrails black from putrefaction, regions where curly poodle fur still remained.

Vince looked at me, confused. He mouthed *what's going on?*

"No," I said. "I'm not going to do it."

Edna protested, said that she couldn't stand the thought of some new family moving in and Puddin' having to spend eternity among strangers.

"It's disgusting to even think about," I said. "You need to just let it go and move on." I felt guilty immediately. After Puddin' died, Edna had declared she'd never own another dog.

Edna sighed. "Well, Gerald told me the young Pinkney couple made an offer on my house," she said. "They want to move in in two weeks. Gerald told me to tell you that you have until then to get Puddin' to the new yard."

Then Edna hung up.

"What was that about?" Vince asked.

I sat back down at the table.

"That was my Aunt Edna," I said. "She wants me to come dig up her old poodle."

Vince's face scrunched together. "What are you talking about?"

I told him the story of Puddin's burial. How, five years before, after a bout of liver cancer, Edna had to have Puddin' put down. And how after that, I dug a three-by-two-foot hole in her backyard and Edna lay Puddin's body in an old burgundy suitcase from Goodwill.

Vince chuckled. "In a suitcase?" he said. "Oh my God, why did you never tell me that before? That's so perfect."

Vince had got a big kick out of my Edna and Puddin' stories: how Edna would, after she'd let Puddin' out to relieve himself, hoist the dog up to her kitchen counter and, with a paper towel, wipe his paws and his butthole. How every Sunday, Edna would slice a week's worth of chicken and mash up some peas and carrots, stick them in the fridge in little Ziploc bags, and, when it was time to feed Puddin', microwave the contents of one baggie for fifteen seconds and serve it to the dog on a tea saucer.

And yet for all the hospice-level care Edna provided Puddin', the dog was a complete menace to the rest of the family. If anyone but Edna went near him, Puddin' would growl, one side of his lip snarling upward, exposing his little pointy teeth (which Edna cleaned with a doggy brush once a week). All of us in the family had been bitten numerous times attempting to crack Puddin's nippy disposition. And each time he bit us, we received a reprimand from Edna for scaring the dog.

"Don't you think you should do it?" Vince asked.

"Are you kidding me? That suitcase probably stinks to high heaven," I said, using a phrase of my mom's.

"Oh, come on, Bobby," Vince said. He brushed his fingers through the waves of hair just above my ear. "It won't be that bad."

Again, I looked at the meatloaf.

I shook my head, brushed Vince's hand away. "It's probably half-decayed," I said. "I don't want anything to do with it."

"It's been five years, hasn't it?" Vince said. "I'm pretty sure it's a skeleton by now."

"I don't know," I said. "Doesn't it take longer to decompose when you put it in a coffin?"

Vince laughed. "Well it's not like you have to open the suitcase."

"That's true," I said, and laughed.

Vince cut a slice of meatloaf—Puddin's head—and set it on my plate.

"I'll help you dig him up," Vince said. "It'll be fun." He stabbed his fork into his own meatloaf slice, chewed a bite. Then he chuckled. "It'll be the last big thing you do before you leave this town."

I laughed uneasily, both at the thought of digging up Puddin' and bringing Vince around Edna. And of leaving Civil Bend. The time was getting close. I'd been collecting cardboard boxes wherever I could get them—from the grocery store uptown, from the United Parish food pantry, from fellow colleagues at the high school. I'd gotten interviews and subsequent offers at two high schools in Sioux Falls to teach history and government.

I cut a little bite of meatloaf, closed my eyes, and stuffed it in my mouth. I chewed, feeling like I'd crossed a minor threshold.

Despite Vince's offer to help me disinter Puddin', I put it off for as long as I could.

A week after the meatloaf supper, Gerald called me, angry.

"What's the matter with you, Bobby?" Gerald asked. "Why don't you just go over there and dig up the damn dog? It'll take you an hour tops."

"That's not the point," I said, matching his angry tone. "The point is that digging up a dead dog is disgusting."

"Well you already buried it once," Gerald said. "What's so bad about doing it again?"

"It's *decayed*, Gerald."

There was a pause. Then a sigh. "Bobby, that dog means the world to her. You know that," Gerald said. "That's why she won't get another dog."

Of course I knew all this. I felt like I knew it better than Gerald.

So I said, "How come I have to do it, then? If you want Puddin' dug up so bad, why don't you come down here and do it yourself? She's *your* mom."

"Bobby, I'm all the way in Minneapolis," Gerald said. "I'm overseeing the renovation of several big properties right now. I can't drive five hours just to dig up an old dog."

"Well it's not like I'm not busy," I said. I glanced at my living room, which was covered in cardboard boxes, some packed and ready to go, others open and spilling over with excess possessions I'd likely leave behind.

"Have you not told your mom yet?" Gerald asked. "You need to tell your mom."

"I'm going to tell her," I said.

After a pause, Gerald said, "You're right there in Civil Bend. You're what, five blocks from Puddin'?"

I didn't say anything. I would've loved nothing more than to have Gerald drive five hours, dig up the Puddin' suitcase, and drive another five hours back.

"You want me to pay you?" Gerald asked. "Is that what this is about?"

I gripped the phone so tightly it hurt my hand.

"Tell you what," Gerald said, "I'll pay you fifty bucks to do it. No. Make it a hundred. Does that sound good? A hundred dollars for an hour's worth of work? I'd say that's better than what they pay you at the school."

I hung up the phone.

Gerald called once more to say that Edna refused to move into the new house unless Puddin' was dug up and brought to the new yard. "This has gone on long enough," Gerald said. "Just do it." For a moment, I saw a grudge-ridden vision of the future in which Gerald and I didn't speak for several years. We'd gather at Christmas for the sake of family peace, sip our Holiday cheer in opposite corners of the room. We'd occasionally make eye contact, then immediately look away.

Still, I stubbornly refused to exhume the poodle—even at the encouragement of my sister, who claimed, conveniently, that she'd drive up from Omaha and do it herself if her son didn't have a soccer tournament that coming weekend.

Finally, my mom showed up one night at supper time to talk me into it. Like her older sister, my mother was still quite stunning at seventy, her wavy black hair only half-peppered, her cheekbones yet high and pronounced, the creases in her olive skin adding a certain dignity to her expressions.

But she, too, was slowing down, her own gait slightly hunched, her stride shortening a bit every year.

"Mom, what are you doing here?" I asked. She hadn't bothered to knock and had instead seen herself through my front door. Such was the way in Civil Bend.

"Bobby, why won't you just go and dig up Puddin' for Edna?" she asked. She hadn't yet noticed the living room with all the boxes.

"Damn it," I said. "That's why you're here?"

"Will you just do it tomorrow? Really, it's the one thing she wants done before she moves."

"How come I have to do everything?" I said, feeling childish even as I said it.

My mom's face tightened. "Edna's very upset with you, Bobby. She expected you to be more understanding."

"What's there to understand?" I said. "The dog's dead. You move on."

We were both silent for several moments. I knew then that I would do it: go back to Edna's yard, exhume the poodle suitcase, and re-bury it. I thought of Edna, how she had lived alone for so long. Sure, I lived alone, too. But I had Vince, which was something—and about to be something more. And so I wondered: was it really that weird of a thing to want your dog's corpse to be near you?

Just then, my mom glanced to her right and saw the boxes. "Bobby, what's all this? Are you moving?" She turned back to me.

"To Sioux Falls," I said. "I'm taking a job at Washington High School."

"Oh."

My mom just stood there, her hands clasped at her chest, like her sister.

"Oh," she said again.

Our eyes met, then we looked away, at the walls or at the kitchen table.

"The pay's better," I added, as if this helped.

My mom nodded. "Well, you certainly want to go where you'll be better compensated."

It was only forty minutes north. Not far, by any means. But far enough that Edna and my mom would have to hire a neighborhood boy to mow the lawn, clean the downspouts, or shovel the driveway in winter. And just far enough that I could have my own life. Not apart from my family. Just my own.

"Listen," I said. "I'll dig up the dog tomorrow."

When she left, I walked my mom to her car, helped her into the driver's seat. Her own decline was sneaking up, subtly but inevitably, like time itself.

As she drove off, I remember thinking that it would somehow be different when the time came to move her out of the two-story house we grew up in. That it would all go very smoothly. Very peacefully.

After all, what else is there to hope for?

The next morning, a Saturday, Vince and I went over to my Aunt Edna's for the last time. On Friday, the movers had transferred what belongings of hers would fit in the new house. Later in the afternoon, Edna would rummage the odds and ends left in the garage. On Monday, the Pinkneys were set to move in.

Sure, I was nervous about facing Edna after our last phone conversation, which had ended with her hanging up on me. And I was fairly certain she'd see through my little lie that Vince was a friend who had come to help me with the digging. She knew all my friends in Civil Bend. Everyone knew everyone's friends in Civil Bend.

We pulled into her driveway and got out of the car. The garage door was open, and Edna was shuffling among the items for the rummage. She saw us approaching and stopped. Her eyes moved back and forth from Vince to me.

"Oh, who's this?" Edna said, her forehead creased in suspicion.

"This is Vince," I said. "He's going to help me dig."

"Oh," Edna said, surprised. Then she smiled—a bit forced, I felt. She said, "I'm so glad you came."

"I'm happy to do it," I said.

The tension wasn't gone exactly. More like pushed to the side, the way it is with families. Edna pointed out two shovels among a pile of tools. Vince and I grabbed one each, and Edna led us to the backyard.

As we walked behind Edna, Vince pinched my shoulder and smiled. For him, this was great fun, getting to see the crazy dog lady in person and digging up the sacred Puddin' corpse. And I couldn't blame him. From a certain, unattached perspective, it was a funny thing we were about to do. So I smiled back, gave Vince a playful jab to the stomach with the handle of my shovel.

Just as before, Edna stood over my shoulder as I dug. In one hand, she held the old white stake, and in the other, a Virginia Slim. With Vince's help, we pierced the suitcase in about ten minutes.

"Oh," Edna said when she heard Vince's shovel make a smacking sound.

Carefully, we removed the earth from around the suitcase. As more and more of it was exposed, I kept waiting for a putrid odor to fill my nostrils. A few times, I thought I detected a foul smell, but it vanished as the light breeze fluttered past.

Finally, the suitcase was uncovered. For a moment, the three of us stood there, gazing down. Its burgundy color had dulled, and a thin, caked layer of dirt covered its casing. I had the silly thought that we were like pirates who had dug up buried treasure. At any rate, the suitcase had a certain power over us—at least it did over me—for it beckoned to be opened.

The force was magnetic. My eyes were drawn to the latches I myself had shut those five years before. I was beyond curious to see what remained of Puddin'.

I turned to Edna. I said, "Okay then. You ready?"

Edna nodded. She dropped her cigarette, stubbed it out.

I grabbed the suitcase and we walked slowly across the backyard, through the garage, and to the driveway. We left the grave unfilled.

I helped Edna into my backseat. She motioned for me to hand her the dirty suitcase, which I did. She set it on her lap. With her right hand, she gripped its handle.

I stuffed the two shovels in the backseat opposite Edna. Then I started my car and pulled onto the street. I glanced at Edna in the rearview mirror. She sat still, gazing out the window at the houses, suitcase in her lap, as if she were going on a trip.

About a block into the five-block drive, I smelled it.

A sour, fruity odor. Immediately, its power churned my stomach. I covered my nose and mouth, as did Vince. From the backseat, Edna coughed.

"Oh my God, roll down the windows," Vince said.

I did, but the pungent, citrusy odor remained. I began coughing, too.

I sped up to thirty-five miles per hour, ten over the in-town speed limit. By the time I pulled into her new driveway, we were all coughing, doing our best to heave breaths through our mouths.

Vince and I leapt out of the car, hacking and fanning the air before our faces. Edna opened her own door, set the suitcase on the driveway.

"Take it, take it," she said.

In the open air, the smell began to dissipate. I took the suitcase, Vince took the shovels.

"Hold on," Edna said, climbing out of the car. "I'm coming."

We walked through the garage and to the backyard. Near the screen doors, Edna had already staked a new wreathed grave marker.

"There," she said, pointing to it.

I set the suitcase a good six feet away from Puddin's new grave. Vince and I dug furiously, aware of the smell's power, worried that it might again revisit us. In five minutes, we'd managed to dig a hole about the same size as Puddin's previous grave.

I shuffled over to the suitcase, grabbed it by the handle, and set it in the new hole.

It fit, snug.

I turned to Edna. "Okay then. Do you want to say anything before we cover him?"

Edna's hands were cupped over her nose and mouth. She shook her head. Quickly, Vince and I re-buried Puddin'. And that was that.

Edna showed us inside, filled us two glasses of water from her kitchen sink.

Vince downed his in one gulp, wiped his mouth with his wrist. We were silent for a moment. Then Vince said, "God, that smell was *awful*."

Edna nodded. "I thought I was going to throw up," she said.

Then we laughed.

Edna showed us around her new place, which had already been furnished and decorated to her specifications by the movers. There was a living room, two bedrooms, two bathrooms, and a kitchen.

After the tour, Edna said, "Hopefully this place is it."

We knew what she meant. Then Edna talked about how grateful she was to have me around to mow her lawn and get her groceries for her. Naturally, I couldn't bring myself to tell her about my own move just then.

And while Edna told Vince about how Civil Bend had shrunk over the years, how there used to be a movie theater uptown and how there was once a clothing store next to the post office, I thought of my own mother. How, if she lived long enough, she'd have to make the same move Edna made.

I felt guilty, as if I were abandoning my aunt and my mother when they needed me most. But again, Sioux Falls was not far. I'd still be closer to them than my sister or Gerald.

As Edna continued talking, I rested my hand on the back of Vince's neck. At first, he stiffened. But when Edna didn't react or comment, he relaxed. We stayed that way for a half hour or so, until it was time to leave.

When we said goodbye, Edna thanked us for helping with Puddin'. Vince and I got in my car, and I kept the windows rolled down just to make sure any lingering remnants of the smell were gone. As we pulled out of the driveway and into the street, I glanced in the rearview mirror.

Edna stood in the driveway, hunched, her hands clasped in front of her chest. Then she turned and shuffled slowly back inside.

COSTUMING

WE DIDN'T WONDER WHAT Jordan's face looked like until after he'd started wearing the prosthetic makeup masks. Before then, none of us knew, that first month of our Makeup Artistry class, that Jordan even existed. Two months in, we learned the process of making prosthetic makeup and had the chance to view our first finished products, which were all individual approximations of the possessed girl's face in *The Exorcist*.

We were allowed a little creative freedom on our moulage, or wounds, and Jordan made a gruesome blackened hole over the bridge of his mold's nose with green gunk oozing forth and another gapingly jagged hole on the left cheek. We all tried our masks on that day—it was tradition to do so after you'd completed a mold. It was obvious that Jordan's mask was of a skill the rest of us didn't yet possess. Some of us complimented him. He didn't speak. Merely nodded. Of course, we all took our masks off and returned the next day bearing our real faces. But Jordan returned in the decaying face of the little devil-possessed girl.

Reactions among us were mixed. Some thought the act was funny and in the spirit of our artistic ambitions, which after all, inhered a certain silliness when you thought about it, the whole notion of creating grisly facial alterations for actresses and actors in movies. Others, however, took Jordan's mask wearing as a boastful gesture, for he had made the best mask, and we would, in the end, be competing against one another in two years' time for limited work on movie sets.

Our instructor, Miss Swanson, was an English ex-pat who spoke with a pleasing British accent. Before Jordan's awesome display of talent, she hadn't said two words to the young man. Now, however, she asked, "Were you in this class before?" Some of us laughed. Others wondered, perhaps a bit uneasily, whether or not he really had been in our class all along.

What really startled us was when Jordan spoke. In the deep, gravelly voice of the demonic girl, he said, "My name's Jordan Sunderland. Check the roster."

"That's a quite good impression," said Miss Swanson. Then she checked the roster and sure enough, he was there.

In the coming days, we worked on our next assignment, which was to mold a *Planet of the Apes*-inspired mask. We were working our way through the classics of prosthetic makeup, following in the footsteps of the pioneers of our art form, artists like John Chambers and Dick Smith. And each day, Jordan came to class with his *Exorcist* face.

In fact, he went everywhere in it. We saw the possessed girl's face in line at the cafeteria breakfast, lunch, and supper. We passed by that face on the sidewalks of our verdant campus, nestled against the San Gabriel mountains just northeast of Los Angeles. We saw that face as we went to and from Victorian Period Costuming or Historical War Setting. The boys in Jordan's dorm hall even saw obscured glimpses of the lurid face in between slits in the shower curtains. Which of course made us wonder if Jordan ever took the mask off. Perhaps, we wondered, he removed it in the privacy of his own room. But we couldn't be sure what went on behind Jordan's closed door, for he resided in one of the few highly sought-after individual dorms.

Jorge Alvidrez, who majored in CGI special effects, said, "What does Jordan's real face even look like?"

We stared at one another, baffled. None of us knew, hadn't thought to know. Indeed, his birth into the world, from our perspective, began with *The Exorcist* mask. Which only made the question burn even fiercer. What *did* his face look like?

Was there, we speculated, some horrible deformity he was covering up? This seemed to us both likely and unlikely. Likely in that why else would he want to cover his face? Unlikely in that surely such a physical aberration would have been noted by someone in that first month of class.

Bettie Hayes piped up. "Maybe he had his hair long. You know, to cover it up."

Which brought us to the question of Jordan's hair. Was it long? Long enough to, say, cover his eyes and nose and mouth? Some remembered it being brown, though this proved unreliable, for others specifically remembered that it was blond.

Sam Bass, a perfectionist of an aspiring film editor, took it upon himself to learn Jordan's schedule and covertly follow him about campus, though it meant Sam having to skip his Action Sequence Editing seminar on Tuesday afternoons. Sam woke early and lurked in the vicinity of Jordan's door, waiting for it to open. Perhaps, Sam conjectured, he'd catch a glimpse of the mysterious young man unmasked, if even for a moment.

As it happened, though, the door would open, but the face was always the Exorcist girl, or, once we'd completed the second assignment, the sneering face of an evil ape. The second mask was constructed with even more skill than the first, more precise in its verisimilitude, with crinkled ape flesh, square rows of bucktooth molars, and forested scraggles of jet-black fur. In fact, it was so realistic that many who glanced casually thought for a second there was actually a bipedal ape in their midst. This illusion was enhanced by Jordan's altered gait, which took on a bent-over, broad-shouldered hunch, more primate than human. Some claimed to have even seen him at times walk on all fours, his weight shifted forward to his knuckles, his wrists bent inward.

Sam Bass tailed Jordan for two weeks. He sat in on Jordan's classes, followed him into the bathrooms, tried to peek under the stall. He stood for untold nocturnal hours outside Jordan's window, peering inside, seeing but not seeing. Jordan just rehearsed his character's actions and speech, over and over for hours. And he was getting really good, Sam claimed. So good that on the last night Sam spied on him, while Jordan slept in the *The Exorcist* mask, a whole demonically possessed episode unfolded, just like in the movie. Jordan's eyes glowed and green bile ejected from his mouth. The bed, Sam shuddered in the retelling, levitated.

We laughed this off, for we knew it to be impossible, the beds in our dorms being soldered firmly to the floor. Be that as it may, after the *Exorcist* incident, Sam Bass gave up his investigation. The project was then taken up by Marjorie Blankenship, something that struck as all as immediately hopeful.

Marjorie was delicately slim, pale-skinned, dark-haired, and always wore black-rimmed glasses. Though friendly and jovial, something of her temperament gave the impression one couldn't ever truly get to the center of her, that there would always be something locked away. In this way, she seemed to us an approximate kindred spirit to Jordan. At any rate, she was very enthusiastic to play the part of an undercover sleuth.

"I will get him to open up," Marjorie promised us. "If that means going on dates and pretending to like him, so be it."

For the first of Marjorie's dates with Jordan, she arranged to meet up for dinner at a local burger joint. Several of us strategically sat in the nearby tables, listening and stealing glances.

By that time, we had completed our third assignment, which were attempts at the 121-year-old face of Jack Crabb, played by Dustin Hoffman in the film *Little Big Man*. While our prosthetic ancient faces were noticeably amateurish, Jordan's was so vividly lifelike that, even as we sat there in the restaurant, knowing full well of the illusory effect, we had to concentrate on the fact that the person eating and conversing with Marjorie was actually our peer and not an impossibly old man.

Jordan's hunchback and painfully slow, brittle movements were utterly convincing. His voice came out hoarse and raspy, as if his vocal chords were on their last legs. Had he, like Dustin Hoffman, screamed at the top of his lungs in his dorm room for one entire hour before this performance? If this was not disturbing enough, for the whole dinner, Jordan played the role of Jack Crabb, and truly, if you've seen *Little Big Man*, he was exactly as Dustin Hoffman portrayed him. He would speak of nothing but his youthful, Wild West misadventures with the Pawnee tribe, his rivalry with Younger Bear, his time as a snake-oil salesman, his ownership of the general store and marriage to a Swedish woman, his friendship with Wild Bill Hickock, his time served in the U.S. 7th Cavalry under General George Armstrong Custer, and his ultimate slaughter-filled deliverance of Custer into the hands of the Sioux at Little Bighorn.

At the end, many of us thought, didn't Jordan look somehow smaller when he stood from his chair to leave? It seemed that, beyond the *Little Big Man* prosthetics and gravelly voice and creaky bodily movements, he'd actually *shrunk* to fit the smaller stature of Jack Crabb.

We decided later, in regard to Jordan's size, that we couldn't know for sure, since no one had thought before to precisely observe his actual height. But we did agree that, in comparison to the *Little Big Man* character, the ape had seemed somehow bigger.

"Maybe he is actually that short," speculated Connie Li, "and for the ape, he just stuffed his shoes with something to make himself look taller."

"I don't know," said Jim Agnew. "When I saw him as the ape, he walked on all fours. It's hard to say if he was taller then or not."

It was around this same time that we noticed supplies missing from the prosthetic makeup cabinet in our classroom. Penny Childress could specifically remember there being six bottles of silicone rubber, which we used to lifecast our faces. But, she pointed out, now there were only four. Darren Adams noticed a few missing boxes of fiberglass bandages—for covering the first flimsy lifecast mold—and Oscar Seinfeld cited a conspicuous depletion of gypsum cement from the large tub. The school kept so much clay on hand it was hard to tell if any was missing, but Annie Potts could swear some was.

Of course it had to be Jordan. If anyone was likely to be crafting prosthetic masks on the side, it was him. A few of us thought we ought to turn him in, but the vast majority were too curious to see what he would do with his extra supplies. We'd already seen him take the art of prosthetic makeup to such heights as to virtually erase the lines between prosthetics and reality. How could anyone blame us for wanting to see what was next?

On the fifth date, Jordan broke from the ape character long enough to invite Marjorie back to his dorm. She nearly spat out her food.

"Yes!" she exclaimed.

Suddenly, however, she turned to us, her face tight in consternation. Was it really a good idea to go back to Jordan's dorm? Wasn't he at least mildly dangerous, given his status as a known thief, and, more importantly, the degree to which he could manipulate reality? Did we really want to accept complicit responsibility for whatever might happen to Marjorie behind Jordan's perpetually closed door?

Of course we didn't want anything bad to happen to Marjorie. But we were dying to know the truth of the matter, and, to be fair, Marjorie had basically said she was willing to do whatever it took to get to the bottom of it. So Marjorie accompanied the ape man back to his dorm that night—the rest of us, as inconspicuously as possible, following not far behind.

After they entered, two teams posted watch, one immediately outside the dorm room door and the other outside the window. The team at the door reported hearing from inside the room, in the first fifteen minutes or so, an exchange of banal pleasantries. But these stopped suddenly, after which there was no audible sound of any kind. The window team said they could see nothing, for the curtains were drawn so tightly as to completely obscure even the smallest glimpse.

We waited, unsure how long it would take. As the hour grew later, some left to go to bed, citing midterm exams the next morning in the notoriously difficult Natural Lighting Seminar, taught by the one of the nation's leading Kubrick scholars, Roberta Ortiz. The rest of us stayed put, too eager to hear, the moment Marjorie emerged, the answer to the mystery.

In the morning, at precisely 7:12 a.m., Marjorie slipped out of Jordan's dorm, closing the door swiftly. She glanced at the small crowd of us and walked briskly away.

"Marjorie!"

But she didn't turn. She disappeared behind the distant corridor. We tried Jordan's door, but it was locked. We pressed our ears against the cheap wood but heard nothing. We knocked, knowing that Jordan was still in the room. We waited there all morning for an answer that didn't come, waited right up until we had to leave to go to Makeup Artistry.

"Did she look different to you guys?" asked Shawna Dressler.

"Yeah," said Aaron Hayes. "Like taller or something."

"Or maybe shorter."

"Maybe a little heavier?"

"No, thinner."

Bleary-eyed and sleep-deprived, we debated on our way to class what Marjorie Blankenship had looked like in the first place. To be sure, we knew her appearance in a general sense—black hair, pale white skin, intellectually suggestive black-rimmed glasses. And the personage that emerged from Jordan's dorm matched that generality. But, we concurred, there was something in each of our guts—call it our intuition—that didn't set right when we saw this version of Marjorie. There was something different about her, some change. We just couldn't put a collective finger on what it was.

Our suspicions rose when Marjorie skipped into class that day. "Hey, guys!" she said, sitting in her usual spot between Tanner Ogden and Rebecca Ramirez. There was something different about her all right, something beyond her sudden gain/loss of weight and increase/decrease in height. Was it her voice?

We hounded her with questions of the previous night. She gave forthright, honest-sounding answers that couldn't possibly be true. For example, she said she and Jordan had watched each of the movies for class: *The Exorcist*, *Planet of the Apes*, and *Little Big Man*. She said that Jordan had removed his mask and that he was actually very handsome, that he looked like a young Brad Pitt in *A River Runs Through It* and that although they didn't share a romantic connection, any girl would be lucky to date him.

"Are you sure?" asked Sam Bass.

"Sure about what?" Marjorie chuckled.

"I don't know," Sam said. "Like everything you just said."

What were we to do? Obviously something was wrong with Marjorie, if this person was in fact Marjorie. We had all been there, listening. They hadn't watched any movies. And there was no way Jordan was, under his mask, in actuality a young Brad Pitt. We didn't realize until after class Jordan's absence that day.

For the next few days, Marjorie nearly drove us crazy. She would come to class as she always did, intellectual glasses and pale skin. She'd sit in her spot between Tanner Ogden and Rebecca Ramirez. She'd work on the next assignment, which was to make a torn-away *Terminator* face, exposing subcutaneous circuitry. She was outwardly cheerful, though slightly guarded, just like she always was. Her movements were exactly as we remembered them, a bit choppy like a stick figure in motion, given her thinness and height. But it all felt wrong. It was right there in each of us, at the base of our guts: a deep, discomforting unease.

Finally, on the third day of this Marjorie charade, Zach Winburn came out and said it. "I don't think it's her. I don't know why. I just don't."

Others agreed. There was some ineffable quality that was off about this version of Marjorie Blankenship. Still, there was a sizable contingency who argued in favor of reason. Based on our senses and our memories, they said, there is no discernable difference between the Marjorie that existed before and the one that exists now. Therefore, there couldn't possibly be some other version of Marjorie—a clone, if in fact that's what the skeptics were suggesting.

"What about Jordan?" asked Jim Agnew. "Where has he been these last few days?"

That no one had an answer for. Not only had Jordan not been in Makeup Artistry, but according to our reliable sources who looked into the matter, he hadn't been in any of his other classes either.

The next day, Marjorie changed yet again. She shuffled into the classroom, stooped and unsteady. She looked deeply weary, utterly exhausted. She sat down between Tanner Ogden and Rebecca Ramirez. Rebecca asked if she was all right. Marjorie didn't answer.

"You look different," said Aaron Hayes.

"Different how?" asked Shawna Dressler.

"I don't know. Just *different*."

After class, we discussed the possibility of now a third Marjorie.

"Are you saying there are more than two Marjories?" asked Jim Agnew.

"Maybe," said Sydney Tarleton. "There was the original, the one that went on that date with Jordan. Then there was the one that came out of Jordan's room. And now there's this one, the tired, lifeless one."

"So what about Jordan? Where is he?"

We had not seen hide nor hair of Jordan all week. His door remained locked. Some had kept watch at the door and window, but these efforts proved futile. We started to wonder if he had dropped out of school.

Marjorie did her best to reintegrate. She initiated conversations, laughed at jokes, tagged along to our group outings. And we did our best to casually accept her. But many remained skeptical. How could we know she was who she said she was? Moreover, there were those who believed she knew something and was holding out on us. She had entered the belly of the beast. We had all seen it. And though she would discuss any number of other topics, on this one point she remained silent.

But then, one by one, it started happening to the rest of us.

One day, Sam Bass was gone from class. The next day he returned, exactly the same but changed. It was just like Marjorie. We knew it as soon as he entered the classroom. Everything about his appearance, his mannerisms, and his voice said Sam Bass. But again that feeling of uncertain wrongness pierced us viscerally.

"Hey, guys," Sam said, pulling up a chair. "What were you talking about?"

Was it his eyes? His mouth? We couldn't decide, but for the next two days, this altered version of Sam Bass inhabited our classroom, our cafeteria, our dorm halls, our minds. Rather than ask him questions, it was easier to ignore him. Some might call it shunning, and I suppose that's what it was. But we all agreed, this other Sam Bass was a pretender, and it was horrifying to have to talk to him. Every basic sensual function told us that it was the real Sam Bass, that it looked like him, sounded like him, smelled like him. But something else, something deeper within us knew this to be a lie, and so talking to him was to be torn in half by these two hemispheres, ripped apart at the center. One couldn't bear it.

In a few days, however, Sam Bass returned the same way Marjorie had. Tired, disheveled, vaguely lost. And, like Marjorie, we didn't trust him. Then it happened to Sydney Tarleton. Shunning her was hard. She was a sweet girl. But what else could we do?

It happened in succession to Connie Li, Aaron Hayes, Shawna Dressler, Tanner Ogden, and Rebecca Ramirez. As the strangeness spread, our class split into those who had changed and those who hadn't.

We stopped talking to the altered, as we began calling them (Marjorie was retroactively shunned). We avoided them in the dorm halls, in the cafeteria lines, at the tables, the restrooms. We treated them as if they had a communicable disease, for we half-believed that's precisely what it was. If, by their subtle manipulation or our own nostalgia, we were sucked into conversation with them, that horrible feeling of being split in half came over us like a raging fever. How could we ever be sure they were who they said they were?

It got so bad that, as our numbers decreased, some of us felt the urge to pull at the cheeks of the altered, hoping to get at their real faces, hoping, once and for all, to know the truth. It was the only way to know, we decided. Shortly before he went to the other side, Jim Agnew did this very thing to Shawna Dressler.

We were in class. Those of us who were still pure sat on the right side of the room. Jim had the last tub of Ultracal-30. He was filling his negative mold with gypsum cement when Shawna casually walked up to him and asked if she could use it when he was done. Jim's eyes bulged, and he lunged at her. He had her on the floor, straddled her. His hands grasped her jawbones, pulling. She screamed. It took three of us to pull him off her, though we'd each later confess, we wished Jim could've kept pulling.

The next day, Jim was gone from class.

Gradually, the altered outnumbered the pure. We stopped looking at one another, for there was no longer any use in doing so. No one's face, it seemed, was their own, and it was only a matter of time before everyone became altered.

My turn finally came. I can only tell it as simply as possible. One night I went to sleep in my dorm and, sometime later, awoke groggily strapped to a wooden chair.

It was all very blurry, and in my memory it still feels more dream than reality. I could see them hanging along the walls, the prosthetic body suits of my peers, flattened like drying laundry. I remember thinking this: that what I saw was the thing we feared most but had never told one another. Underneath, he was all of us. We were costumes that he wore. A wardrobe. I saw us hanging along the walls.

The artist was next to me, stooped over his workbench. The supplies were all there, scattered haphazardly about the bench's surface. I watched as his delicate fingers worked keys along the paper-thin edges of his newest prosthetic mold. Occasionally, he'd glance over his shoulder, and I would see the swirled vortex of facial features, slightly out of focus in my drugged state. He muttered things under his breath in myriad voices—Shawna's, Jim's, everyone's. As he worked, I envisioned the suits around me, one by one, coming to life and speaking, moving about cheerfully. In this vision, everything was restored to the way it was before.

I returned to class the way we all had, which is to say, alone. I took my seat, my head hung. I didn't look at anyone else, and no one looked at me. It just wasn't something we did anymore. Occasionally, I'd catch a glimpse of someone in my peripheral, maybe Jim Agnew or Marjorie Blankenship. The horrible fever would come on, accompanied by a desire to pull at their face. Just to see what was under there. Just to be sure. But I shook this off. Instead, I touched my own jawline, tugged a little. Then a little harder. Only skin. Real skin. I felt momentarily reassured. I'd go back to work on the next assignment, and I'd get to wondering: how do I know for sure?

No one was anyone anymore, it seemed. We had the same life in us as before, but we couldn't bear to share it. So we poured our energy into our work. We'd stop intermittently to pick at our faces. We made other faces. One by one, we took bathroom breaks to stare at our faces in the mirror.

On the last day of class, Miss Swanson spoke in a voice we'd never heard before.

"It's been great working with you this semester," she told us with no trace of her English accent. She cleared her throat and continued, her accent restored, "And as much as I'd love to have you all in Advanced Makeup Artistry next semester, I'm afraid I won't be returning."

We stared at her, the fever coursing our bodies. We all thought the same thing: Miss Swanson isn't Miss Swanson anymore.

"I've taken a job as a prosthetic makeup artist at a new studio in Century City," Miss Swanson explained. "They liked my *Exorcist* and ape and *Terminator* samples." Miss Swanson smiled. "They've already produced Scorsese and Tarantino, to name a few."

Without another word, she walked out of the classroom. For several moments, it was silent.

Then Jim Agnew said, "Were her eyes always that blue?"

Connie Li said, "I thought they were green."

"Weren't they hazel?" asked Rebecca Ramirez.

But there was no way of knowing.

SYMPTOMS

THE POT BROWNIES BELONG to our friends, the Brewsters. I see them in their fridge when I get more iced tea. Though we aren't particularly close, we're over at their house for a dinner party, a monthly thing some of the youngish couples at our church do. We're the last to leave. Anna, my wife, keeps talking to Penelope Brewster about a new rule at the Sioux Falls high schools banning girls from wearing yoga pants.

I'm stuck talking to Doug Brewster one-on-one, which I resent because he speaks only of drywall, something I tried once to patch but failed. Yet he makes good money, enough to put his kids in private Christian school, which is more than Anna and I can afford. I keep glancing at Anna across the living room, tilting my head in the direction of the front door. She nods, the sides of her blonde bob brushing her cheeks. But she continues her discussion.

Twenty minutes later, just as we're leaving, Anna asks if we can take two of the brownies from the fridge. I want to say no, we're good on pot brownies for now, thank you. But I think Doug Brewster is half-ashamed he still dabbles after marriage and a family, after turning his life, ostensibly, over to Christ. He jumps at the opportunity to drag anyone else down his Almost-Forty Pothole, if I can call it that.

At least that's how I choose to view his enthusiasm when his eyes light up and he says, "Sure, come on."

We eat them together, Anna and I, right there in the kitchen in front of Doug and Penelope. It reminds me of how, when I was a kid, my Grandma used to force-feed me homemade sweets every time we visited. She, too, would watch me eat her brownies, which she sprinkled with powdered sugar. She'd stare at me intently, wouldn't relax until I nodded approvingly and went "Mmmm."

"You should start feeling it about the time you get home," Penelope says.

This is because the Brewsters live in a nice old Victorian on the Northside of Sioux Falls, whereas we live twenty miles south of town in one of the many suburban developments that are proliferating like bacteria cultures.

On the drive home, Anna starts giggling, even before either of us feel anything. We zip past downtown, past the mall at the southern edge of town. Then we're past all the lights, past everything, and it's just the South Dakota prairie darkness, which is like the darkness of being stuffed in the trunk of a car.

I get paranoid about my circulation, so I keep cupping my hand over my chest, feeling my heartbeat for any increase in tempo, any skips. Any irregularities of any kind.

The last time we did pot was two years before the Brewster party. We got tickets to an Eric Clapton concert. Once again, it was Anna's spontaneous idea.

"Wouldn't it be fun to be high for Eric Clapton?" she said. "We'd be like hippies."

That time, I got the pot from Tim Hayden. He used to work for me. He was older, close to sixty. I offered to pay him, but he refused.

"The first time's always free," he said. Then he ran his hand through his oily hair.

He didn't get fired or anything. My company went under. Premier Mortgage, it was called. I really thought I'd succeed with all the suburban growth around Sioux Falls. I got approved for a fat, quarter-of-a-million-dollar loan. Paid six months' rent on an office space right off South Main downtown. Hired five employees. Had a blue, illuminated sign over the door with a little house logo and everything.

I don't know why it didn't work out, why we couldn't get loans for anyone. Maybe because I hired people like Tim Hayden. Maybe because, in a very real sense, I suck at brokering mortgages.

We went broke in five months. Many days, in the month after I'd let everyone go, I sat by myself in the conference room, pouring shots of bourbon into my Premier coffee mug. I stared at the whiteboard on the wall, which still had bullshit I'd written in green marker: Debt to Income. Loan to Value. Some other worthless phrases: Consistent Professionalism. Eye Contact.

I wanted to blame the housing market at large. But the recession didn't hit Sioux Falls. The market only grew. People bought houses left and right. Anna and I did, which we were now probably going to have to sell at a loss. Or let it get repossessed, which happened to the only three people I got loans for with Premier.

Here's what I told myself: you suck at this.

Still, I got a job with some small, shit bank. I'd never even heard of them, and Sioux Falls isn't that big a place. I work straight commission, which is bad because anyone who gets sent to my desk doesn't want to use my services. They're like: I don't need you. I can get a better deal somewhere else. And I'll say: No, wait, though they're right. I'll even hold my hand out, grasping, but they'll have left.

I keep my old Premier coffee mug in my drawer. When no one's around, I get it out and look at it. Sometimes, I even pretend to take sips, imagining the imagined good old days.

Sometimes I think a name that referenced something local would've fostered success: Dakota Mortgage. Sioux Something or Other. Whatever the Fuck.

When we get home, we're both starting to feel the brownies kicking in. I'm pressing my hand to my chest, almost certain my heartrate is quickening. Anna snaps out of giggle-mode and puts on a serious face for the babysitter. She's a high school girl from somewhere, I don't know. Anna handles the babysitter hires. Scrutinizes their online babysitter profiles and all that.

"They're both asleep, Mrs. Wentz," the girl says.

Anna thanks her, then gives me the look that means I'm supposed to take out my wallet. I do, and hand the girl a twenty and a ten.

"Give her a little more," Anna says.

"I only have a twenty," I say.

"That's fine," Anna says.

I give her a look that's supposed to say: we can't afford this. To which Anna scowls. I relent, and hand the girl another twenty.

As soon as she's out the door, Anna bursts into laughter. That's what she did at the Eric Clapton concert, laughed at everything Clapton did, whether it was play a solo or say the word cocaine, which are the entire lyrics to one of his songs.

"Oh my God!" Anna says, collapsing on the couch. "Do you think she knew?"

"Knew what?"

"That we're high!"

Anna's eyes are now red, which is something I've always found weird. If someone stabs your eye with a pen, it makes sense that it gets red. But from smoking something or eating a brownie? I don't get it.

Anna wants to go check on the girls, which I think is a good but terrifying idea because what if they wake up and want to talk to us?

First, we look in Cassie's room. She's eight. She sleeps facedown with her limbs splayed, as if she's trying to swallow the mattress with her body. She's smart. When the time comes, I'm sure she'll go to college.

Anna hovers over her. She looks back at me and whispers, "That's our daughter."

I don't know what to say. My face burns. I know for a fact my heart is pumping harder than normal. I can feel it without even having to touch my hand to my chest. It gets worse when I think of how, one year ago, I promised Cassie I'd pay for her college. I said it with supreme nonchalance, like it wouldn't be any harder than getting her an ice cream cone. Maybe I'll get lucky and she won't remember in ten years.

Anna leads us into Sierra's room. She's six. She's a troubled kid. She's scared of everything, doesn't like to talk to any other kids. She'll probably wake up soon from a horrible dream. The last one she had, we were all in the car and we got lost and couldn't find our way back home. Of course, in the dream, I was driving, which felt accusatory when Sierra explained it to us.

We go back to the living room. Anna wants to make popcorn and watch a movie. We pop a bag in the microwave and hunker down into the couch, settling on something stupid about a guy who takes a girl home to meet his parents, but his parents are vampires. We devour the popcorn and pop another bag and devour that one, too.

It's not long before Anna gets up from the couch and says, "I'm going to bed."

I feel like I'm at my desk at the shit bank. I reach out my hand. "Wait," I say.

But she's down the hall, gone. It's just me.

Two months ago, I went to Home Depot. Anna wanted new tile on the bathroom floor. She wanted to hire someone to do it. We couldn't afford the tile, let alone afford to pay someone to install it. So we compromised: I would lay the tile myself.

I really thought I could do it. I looked up all the steps on the internet. I made a list of all the supplies. I even knew exactly how many six-inch academy grey porcelain mosaic tiles I'd need to cover the twenty-six square feet of bathroom flooring: 104.

I had to take Sierra with me to Home Depot because Anna had taken Cassie to her Saturday morning soccer practice. Everything went fine at first: we wandered around the store, made a kind of game out of taking items from the shelf and placing them in the cart. Then we got the tile itself. All told, the total came to $526.17. I was almost embarrassed by it. As they swiped my credit card, I thought of all the stuff you could get with five hundred bucks: a cheap laptop, new clothes for the girls, a Model-T in 1925, five hundred cans of soda. I mostly thought about these things to avoid worrying about the card being declined, in which case I'd give them one of the newer cards, one that hadn't been maxed out.

Just before we left, I announced to Sierra that I was going to use the restroom. It was a twenty-five-minute drive home. I admit: not a tortuous length of time to hold back pee. Still, I figured: the restroom's right here by the store's exit; it'll take me thirty seconds; I won't even wash my hands.

"Can I come with?" Sierra asked.

She used to always come with. It wasn't a big deal. She'd stand in the stall with me, face away and towards the door. When we washed our hands, none of the men were weird about it. Other parents did it. I'd seen moms take their little sons into the women's restrooms all the time.

But in that moment, I told myself: six is too old. I don't know why I thought this. Maybe because Sierra was in kindergarten now, public school being the line of demarcation between going to the restroom with your dad and going it alone.

"No," I said. "Just stay right here by the cart. Count to thirty."

Then I turned and hurried into the restroom.

I didn't actually time myself. I did my business as fast as I could, zipped up and made my way back out. It might've been longer than thirty seconds. But there's no way it was longer than a minute.

Outside, Sierra bawled into the arms of a woman wearing an orange Home Depot apron.

All around, people stared: from the checkout line, from the nearby paint section. An older couple walked through the automatic sliding doors and saw Sierra crying. Their faces immediately tightened into concern, compassion.

I approached Sierra and the Home Depot woman. Sierra wailed, "I want to go home!"

"I'm her dad," I said.

But I said it too softly. Or maybe I didn't say it at all. My face burned so hot I could feel prickles on my cheeks. I know in my head I asked: why are you doing this? And I don't know if I was talking to Sierra or myself. The woman kept looking around: at the doors, the checkout lines, the paint section. It's like I wasn't even there.

"It's okay," the woman said, and she rubbed Sierra's shoulder.

Another employee came jogging over, an older bald guy. He looked like maybe he was a manager, eager to put out the kid fire.

Before he could reach us, I stepped in.

"I'm her dad," I snapped.

I took hold of Sierra's hand, gripped it tighter than I should have. I don't know. There were so many damn people. More people came in the store, more people stared. It felt like an encroaching mob.

"Come on, let's go home."

I tugged at Sierra's arm. The woman let go and Sierra came with me. With one hand, I pushed the cart. With the other, I held Sierra's hand. I didn't look back. I stared straight ahead. I didn't want to see the way anyone was looking at me.

Alone, I can't concentrate on the vampire parent movie. I only think of my heartbeat, which is like a jackhammer in my chest. I don't think I'm getting enough oxygen from each breath, so I breathe in deeply, like they tell you to at the doctor's. Still, it's like there's a blockage. Or maybe there's something inside me siphoning off oxygen. Like an oxygen parasite. Do they have those?

I get up from the couch, head down the hall, and go into the bathroom. I turn on the light and shut the door, safe from any peering eyes. I lock it just to make sure.

The concrete, mostly untiled floor is cold on my feet, which actually feels good right now. There are eight academy grey porcelain mosaic tiles I managed to lay against the wall beneath the towel rack. But I fucked it up and they're warped, protruding in spots like they have little tumors. The rest of the tiles are stacked behind the toilet, gathering dust along with the trowel, the level, and the carpenter's square.

I position myself in front of the mirror. I am immediately frightened by my own eyes. They're so bloodshot, the only thing I can compare them to are freshly slit wrists, little trails of blood snaking in all directions over my cornea (or is it under?). I close them tightly, venture deep inside my inner self for a few immeasurable moments. I wait for something big to pop into my head, a truth or a realization. Or God's voice. Or just a thought. I'll even take a thought.

And then it comes: a sudden burst of inspiration to lay tile. I'm so excited by the idea of finishing something I started that it feels like the solution to everything, the chance, at long last, to make things right.

I don't even put on the gloves and goggles. I just grab the trowel and start slapping down grout. I remember from the internet that grout is a powerful bonding agent. I don't even give a fuck where I spread it, so long as it covers the cement. I don't let it dry, if that's what you're supposed to do. I don't know. I slap the mosaic tiles down and press, quickly, as if I'm the guy in the Poe story who walls the other guy in.

I do this over and over, grout and slap, grout and slap. I gain a sense of momentum while simultaneously sweating bullets and pushing my heartrate into what feels like the stratosphere. I remember reading something once about flow, a state where you're so involved with some action you forget yourself. I want to reach flow state by laying tile. As I spread more grout, I think: maybe this is my vocation. Who knew I just had to be high to find my life's calling? I smile, imagining myself buying a truck and adding decals with my business along the sides. I will call it Premier Flooring in honor of my first failed business.

Then I slice my left index finger with the edge of the trowel.

A sharp pain throbs along my finger's last crease, and I cry out in a high, animalistic yelp. It reminds me of the sound my childhood dog made when he stepped in broken glass. It also reminds me of when we put the dog down a few years later because he kept peeing on the furniture. Blood comes streaming out. It looks like my finger had its throat cut.

Both my hands burn from the grout. But the cut is something else. I can tell the situation is bad based solely on the screaming pain raging from my finger's jugular. I do something smart, which is wash my hands in the sink.

Then I don't know to do. My finger still bleeds profusely. And it radiates waves of hot pain far more powerfully than a finger should be allowed to. I grab the toilet paper, unspool a few feet, and wrap it around the wound. I glance back in the mirror. My eyes are still blood red, maybe even bloodier than before. My heart smacks the walls of my chest. My breath is short. Muffled waves sound in my ears like I have seashells cupped over them.

I think: what if you're dying?

I shut the light off and try to open the bathroom door in the darkness, forgetting that I locked it. I jerk at the handle, plunge my shoulder against it, try to break it open. I freak myself out thinking about how when we were in junior high people would stand in front of bathroom mirrors in the dark and say Bloody Mary over and over.

I say Bloody Mary but nothing happens, though I don't wait that long, either.

Then I turn on the light and unlock the door. I dash to the

living room. I get on my phone with my good hand. I don't know what to search for first, stroke or heart attack. Convinced I'm having one or both, I search and select those symptoms that apply to my current situation: fatigue and chest tightness (heart attack); dizziness and confusion (stroke). And the pain in my finger shoots up my arm, or at least I think it does, which according to the search counts towards heart attack.

I have no choice. I dial 9-1-1. I'm a dead man otherwise.

The guy asks me my emergency, and I say stroke and heart attack. He tells me to pick one, and I say heart attack. I don't say anything about the pot brownies. Or the sliced finger. Or the academy grey porcelain mosaic tiles. He says an ambulance can get me in ten minutes. I tell him I hope I can stay alive for that long.

When I hang up, there's a little girl standing in the hallway, wiping at her eyes.

"Daddy?" she says. She comes towards me. "I had a bad dream again."

All I can say about Anna is that things aren't the way they used to be. Sex, when it happens, is weird. Each time, it's like we're two out-of-shape people forcing ourselves to work out. Which is to say: it's not that enjoyable and in some ways it's painful. I know for a fact Anna doesn't enjoy it for the following two reasons:

Exhibit A: the last time we actually had sex, which was six months ago, she literally reached over to the nightstand, mid-act, and checked her phone for any new messages.

Exhibit B: the last time I tried to have sex with her, which was one month ago, I got as far as a hand on her breast before she said, "Let's not."

Which is not to say sex is everything. I jerk off regularly, which is okay for now, I guess. Maybe we're just on our way to becoming one of those married couples who don't have sex (i.e. married couples). Maybe we're on our way to getting divorced as soon as the kids leave the house. Maybe she already has someone on the side. I don't know.

Each day is the same. We come home from work and eat supper. We chew our goulash and listen to the girls tell us about school, which for me is exciting because I hate my job. The girls run off and do whatever after supper. Anna and I settle into the living room and turn on the TV. But we don't watch it. We just play on our phones until we nod off. It usually takes us about two hours.

I mostly play this game where you are an empire and you try to conquer other empires. It's a fantasy I've had ever since, as a boy, I learned about Genghis Khan. I've since forgotten everything I learned about Genghis Khan except that he had more land than anyone at the time. So that's what I try to do.

I don't know what Anna does on her phone. Once, she left it lying on the couch when she went to use the bathroom. I checked it, and there were so many different windows open I couldn't scroll through all of them before I heard the toilet flush.

It could be worse, I suppose. I'm not really sure how, but that's what my dad always used to say. He died at fifty-six of colon cancer.

Here's something I'll never forget: on our honeymoon, Anna and I drove to Wisconsin Dells. Most people outside the Midwest haven't heard of it because it's not actually that cool, not compared to the Rocky Mountains or one of the oceans. We stayed in this log cabin in the woods and on the first night, after a couple bottles of wine, Anna said, "Let's make a baby."

I'd heard people use this exact expression in several movies, and I'd always hated it. But when Anna said it, I was suddenly in awe of the fact that such a thing was possible, that two people could come together and literally make another person. Even though we'd covered the process, step by step, in seventh grade health class, it still seemed miraculous.

That's what we did that night. That's when Cassie was conceived.

So if nothing else, there's at least that between Anna and me: we literally made two other people.

Sierra's dream was about falling off the roof. She was dangling from the downspout, holding on with one hand. I was up there, too. But—big surprise—I failed to grab hold of her hand, and she fell.

"It was like at Home Depot when you did grab my hand, except the opposite," Sierra says.

"Why were you on the roof?" I ask.

"And I fell and fell and kept falling," Sierra explains.

"But why were you on the roof?"

Sierra gasps.

"What happened to your hand?" she asks. "Daddy, you're bleeding. Have you been crying? Your eyes are all red."

I turn away so she can't see my face. This is what it must be like for Doug Brewster every night when he tucks his kids into bed.

The ambulance should be here any minute. I feel as if the moment is upon me to explain to Sierra all the things I want her to know should I not make it through the night.

I face her and say, "Sierra, give me your hand."

She looks worried. Probably because I'm bleeding and my eyes are red and I didn't explain why. Nevertheless, she offers me her right hand. With my good hand, I take it and press it to my chest.

"Do you feel that?" I ask.

"It's beating fast," she says.

I nod. Then I try to think of something I want her to know. In the distance, I hear the faint tones of the ambulance siren.

"People do things in life," I say, not sure where I'm going next. "You see, because at the end of the day, when the sun sets, it's not actually the end of, well, it's the end of that day, but it's also actually a new day on the opposite side of the world."

"Because of the earth spinning!" Sierra says. "Miss Gomez taught us that."

The siren gets a little louder. Sierra looks over her shoulder. I squeeze her hand, and she turns back to me.

"That's right," I say. "But that's not everything. You see, there's the stuff they teach you in school, and then there's the stuff they teach you in—"

"In the Bible?"

"No. Well, yes, the Bible. But there's also life, which isn't like the movies. You probably think life is like the movies."

Sierra shrugs and turns in the siren's direction, which is now only blocks away. I have no idea what I'm saying. If I do die, I will have left her only debt, which is actually worse than nothing. The kids who get left nothing are lucky in this sense.

I pull Sierra into me and hold her. I don't say anything, banking on the cliché about actions over words. I don't think it really works. Sierra pulls away and says, "There's an ambulance out front."

We both go to the door. I open it, and we step outside.

The siren is so loud and shrill it's almost like a weapon. It might knock us over if we're not careful. Neighbors' lights are turning on left and right.

I crouch down to Sierra.

"I have to go," I say. "If your mother wakes up, tell her I had to go to the ER."

"The ER?"

"She'll know what I mean."

I stand, make my way down the stoop and towards the ambulance. An EMT climbs out and looks me over. He seems suspicious.

"Are you the guy having a heart attack?"

I hold up my hand, wrapped in toilet paper, as if called on by the teacher.

"I am him," I say.

The whole thing is a big mistake. I realize this when we're almost to the hospital and I don't feel very high anymore and remember

I don't have health insurance. I tell them I'm actually okay now, though my finger throbs, and maybe I could just come back tomorrow during regular hours.

But they lead me down the white-walled hallway and stick me in a room. I have to take off my shirt and climb into the bed and have all the sticky things attached to my chest. Meanwhile, a nurse cleans out my finger and says I need a few stitches. She applies a local anesthetic, then sews me up while the machine to my right beeps.

A few minutes later a doctor comes in. He's middle-aged, maybe fifty. He looks pissed. He glances over the results of my ECG, which causes him to look even more pissed.

"There's nothing wrong with you," he says. "Why did you think you were having a heart attack?"

"Doctor, I looked up my symptoms on the internet, and they matched the symptoms of a heart attack," I say.

"The internet is a cancer," the doctor says. Then he leaves the room.

I've never heard a doctor call something a cancer that wasn't cancer. It's something to think about. It's worth wondering if doctors call other non-disease things diseases, too.

On my way out, a woman hands me a bill for $4,264.43. Most of it's from the ambulance ride. I try to think of all the things one could get with four thousand dollars, but I mostly think of cheap, used cars.

"Do I have to pay this right now?" I ask.

"No," the woman says.

So I walk out the hospital's doors.

Outside, the twilight air is crisp and cool. It reminds me of brisk mornings when, as a boy, I walked to school with a Ninja Turtles backpack slung over my shoulders. I had a lot going for me back then. I was like Sierra, except without all the fear and bad dreams.

I stuff the hospital bill in my pocket when I see Anna pull up in our Ford Focus. I did not call her, but she has come. I suspect Sierra, who sits in back with her sister and looks wide awake, relayed the message.

Anna rolls down the window.

"Get in," she calls.

I know I will get in the car and we'll drive home and things will be as they were before, only a little worse. I've always known I'll get in the car and go back home, even in my Ninja Turtle backpack-wearing days. When I was a boy, there was always a car, and it was always waiting, and I always got in it.

I get in this one. There is a woman next to me and two girls in back.

It's a while before anyone says anything.

RANSOM

JACOB CARBUNKLE JOINED OUR seventh-grade class three weeks before the Milburn's three-year-old son was kidnapped. He told us his parents were going to do it because that's what they did for a living.

There were fifteen of us seventh graders, and in our little town, we'd never had a new student. On the first day of school, our teacher, Mrs. Douglas, stood with Jacob at the front of the room. Even she didn't seem to know what to do or what to make of the new student.

"Class," Mrs. Douglas said. "This is, um, Jacob Carbunkle."

Beanpole thin, Jacob's stringy hair draped past his eyes. We couldn't see much of his face. He shook his head, and his bangs parted like curtains. For a moment we saw his grey eyes.

Cain Sanders muttered, "Are we supposed to say hi?"

Mrs. Douglas said, "Jacob, would you like to tell us a little about yourself?"

Jacob shrugged and said, "I'm from North Dakota. It's really cold up there." He paused for a moment. Then his index finger popped up, as if he'd remembered something. "Oh yeah, my parents own their own business and they work from home. It's a kidnapping business."

We looked to Mrs. Douglas. She removed her glasses. She

rubbed her eyes with her thumb and index finger. Then she put her glasses back on and chuckled. Then she told Jacob to take a seat in the back. He sat next to Ted Gunderson and Marissa Schmitz.

"He said it's a really simple business: his parents kidnap the kid and get money and then give the kid back," Marissa told us at lunch.

"It's like you steal something and then sell it back to the person you stole it from," said Ted Gunderson.

We nodded. It seemed simple enough.

Marissa said, "He told us he would babysit and collect data on the kids."

"Data?" we asked.

"Yeah, like height and weight and whether or not they minded his commands," Ted explained. "And how long they like to watch cartoons for. And how quiet they can be for long periods of time."

We laughed. We thought: We've never heard of pieces of data like this.

"That's what he said," Marissa said. Then she shrugged.

Those first few days, Jacob sat at a table alone in the corner of the lunchroom. He stooped over his tray like our grandparents at the nursing home. We figured he was waiting for us to come to him.

So in a spirit of inclusiveness, we invited him to Josephine Reynolds' thirteenth birthday party, which was being held at her house that Friday.

"Really?" he said. He looked up at us. His bangs parted. Patches of red pimples dotted his jawline. "Does Josephine have any younger siblings?"

We told him she had a five-year-old brother named Tyler. He said that was pushing it on the upper-age limit.

"Do Josephine's parents make a lot of money?" Jacob asked.

We told him her mom was a CPA and her dad delivered mail on county rural routes.

"I'd love to come," Jacob said.

Josephine's party was par for the junior high course. Her parents parked their cars on the street and cleared space in the garage for a dance floor. Josephine had a dance playlist all set up on Spotify, intermixed with slow songs. At first, we sat on the foldout chairs, eating chips and salsa and drinking soda. Incrementally, we took to the dance floor. Every half hour or so, Josephine's parents would peek in, scan the scene, then wave goodbye.

Jacob didn't dance. He stayed seated in a chair talking to Josephine's little brother, Tyler. Jacob would·gesture wildly, as if emphasizing high points in a story, and Tyler would laugh. Once, Sally Winters asked Jacob to dance during a slow song, and he said no, he needed to collect more data on Tyler.

"Jacob is really good with kids," Katie DeLong said.

"Do you think his parents will kidnap Tyler?" Kim Oberly teased.

We looked at Josephine, the birthday girl. "That's a good one, Kim," she said uneasily.

"I bet he'd make a really good father," said Bobby Sellers.

The following Thursday, Jacob wasn't in school.

That was the day Billy Milburn turned up missing at the grocery store.

It was completely inexplicable. That's the word Sally Winters told us her mom used.

The story went like this: Gary Milburn was grocery shopping with Billy, he and Mandy's three-year-old son. He pushed his cart through the canned foods aisle. Billy followed closely behind, running his fingers along the edges of the shelves. It was how Gary and Billy always grocery shopped. Gary stopped to consult his list. His eyes moved back and forth from the list to the shelf. Then he reached forward and grabbed a can of kidney beans. When he turned back to the cart, Billy was gone.

Gary ran around the store, calling Billy's name. He was nowhere to be found. No fellow customer or employee had seen the little boy. The parking lot was empty save for three cars, one of which was Gary's.

"Are you sure you even brought Billy with you?" Mark Munger, the store owner, is said to have asked Gary.

Two days before Billy disappeared, Jacob told us at lunch that it would happen. He said, "My parents are going to kidnap the little Milburn boy."

We weren't sure we'd heard him right. So we asked him to repeat what he'd said.

"The Milburn boy," Jacob said. "His parents run the bank. You see, in kidnapping, the risk is high, so you want the reward to be worth it. So you always target the people with the most money."

We were silent. Then Connor Billings said, "That makes sense. From a financial standpoint, I mean."

We looked at each other. We had more questions.

"When are they going to do it?"

"This Thursday," Jacob said. "Mr. Milburn takes his son grocery shopping on Thursday afternoons. The store's usually almost empty."

"Then what?" said Marissa Schmitz. "I mean, what do you do after you kidnap him?"

Jacob pushed his bangs out of his eyes. He looked at Marissa like she was stupid. "You write a ransom note."

"Like with letters cut out of a magazine and glued together?" asked Shane Livingston.

Jacob shook his head. "My parents use an old typewriter."

"Where do they keep him?"

"In the basement."

"For how long?"

"Until they deliver the requested amount of money to the agreed-upon location."

All the adults of our town joined in the search. Our parents scoured the park, the playgrounds, the little tree groves surrounding the trailer courts. They searched under the bushes and evergreens of innocent neighbors. They checked the dugouts of the baseball fields, the sand traps of the golf course, the rows of cornfields at the edge of town. Geoff Olsen even took his boat ten miles up and down the nearby Sioux River, using his side-scan sonar system to see if little Billy had sunk to the bottom.

Jacob's stick-figure parents joined in the search—a maneuver necessary not to arouse suspicion, Jacob told us. They walked next to Mark Munger, the grocery store owner. Occasionally, the three of them would stop to discuss something. Mr. Munger's eyes would scan the other searchers. Then they'd keep walking.

We joined in the search, too. We walked next to Jacob, eager for any details he was willing to disclose.

"So how'd you do it?" asked Bobby Sellers. "I mean like, how'd you pull it off?"

Jacob pointed at his parents and Mr. Munger. "Well, you see the grocery guy? He's in on it. He made sure to distract the few customers who might have seen anything. Then my mom nabbed little Billy when Mr. Milburn wasn't looking. She ran with him to the parking lot, where my dad was waiting in a junk car they bought solely for this purpose. Then they drove off."

"What'd you do?" asked Marissa Schmitz.

"I was at the edge of the parking lot on my bike, keeping watch," Jacob said. "If any car came by, I'd give my dad the signal."

"What's the signal?" asked Ted Gunderson.

Jacob whirled his hand above his head in a spiral.

We nodded approvingly. It was a good signal.

The Milburns received their ransom note two days after Billy disappeared. It was typed on old, yellowed paper in Courier font.

"You always want to wait at least a day before delivering the ransom note," Jacob explained at lunch.

"Why?" Cain Sanders asked.

Jacob shrugged. "It's just what my parents say. I think it's to allow desperation to sink in, so that they'll be more willing to pay."

Jacob's parents were asking for ten million dollars.

"My parents said there aren't even ten million dollars in our town's bank," said Bobby Sellers.

"You always ask high," said Jacob.

"Ask high?"

Jacob nodded. "You intentionally ask for more than they can pay. Then they get on the news and say they don't have that kind of money. Then they tell you how much they can pay, and you take that."

"I get it," said Connor Billings. "It's like a business negotiation."

"Exactly," Jacob said. Then he looked at Connor. "You'd be good at this."

We looked at Connor. His cheeks reddened. He shifted in his seat.

"I don't know," Connor said. A tiny smile formed at the corners of his mouth. "Maybe."

The search had gone on for one week when we asked Jacob if we could see little Billy.

"I mean, he's in your basement, right?" asked Josephine Reynolds.

Jacob nodded. "He's probably watching cartoons right now. Or maybe my mom is reading Dr. Seuss books to him. Or maybe he's taking a nap."

"So can we see him?" asked Ted Gunderson.

"That'll be hard," Jacob said.

"How come?"

"Because my parents are always home now," Jacob said. "They won't let me have anyone over when we've got a kid in the basement. If you would've asked a week ago, you'd have been welcome to come over."

We sighed.

Then Jacob's index finger popped up. "But I could sneak a few of you in at night. Only like three or four. Five at the most."

We looked at one another.

"What's the fairest way to decide?" asked Sally Winters.

The Milburns appeared on the six o'clock news. It was a station out of Platte Lake, the only town of any size in our vicinity. We watched over supper with our families.

"We just want our little boy back," said Gary Milburn, his eyes red and bleary.

"We'll pay," said Mandy Milburn. "We'll pay all we can." Then she broke down and sobbed on her husband's chest.

Gary held up his right hand, open-palmed. "We'll pay five million. I know it's five less than they're asking for, but we just don't have that kind of money."

We seventh graders chewed our meatloaf, our scalloped potatoes, our green bean casseroles. We nodded and thought: *Ask high.*

On the second Saturday after the kidnapping, Jacob snuck five of us in through the back door and into the kitchen. He had to unlock the door leading down to the basement.

It was an unfinished basement, with concrete walls and floors. They had set up a small living space for little Billy: a couch, a rug, a television, a box of toys in one corner, a pile of Dr. Seuss books in the other.

Jacob pointed to the blowup mattress next to the toys. On it, a lumpy little figure laid motionless.

"That's him," Jacob said.

We squinted, not able to see very well in the darkened basement. We couldn't be sure, but the figure looked more like little pillows stuffed under a blanket than a little boy.

"So he just stays here all day?" asked Sally Winters.

Jacob nodded. "He's a very well-behaved child."

"Doesn't he ask about his mom and dad?" asked Ted Gunderson.

"Sure," Jacob said. "But we just tell him they're on vacation and that they're bringing him back something special. You always want to give the child something to look forward to. It keeps them placated."

We didn't know what that word meant, but we nodded. It was a good word.

Just then, we heard footsteps upstairs. Then the basement door opened.

Jacob shuffled us off to a dark corner beneath the stairs.

"Who's there?" a woman's voice called. She descended the stairs. "Billy? Are you up?"

"It's just me," Jacob said. He met the woman at the base of the stairs. "I was just checking on Billy."

"Oh," she said. "Well I have to be at the church early in the morning. Ethel can't play piano. She's sick. I thought I'd just stop by now and drop off some new books."

"Thanks," Jacob said.

From our vantage point, we could see the woman hand Jacob a stack of hardcover books.

The woman said, "How's he doing?"

"Fine," Jacob said. "Did you see the news the other night? It shouldn't be too much longer."

The woman nodded. "Okay then," she said. She turned and walked back up the stairs.

When she'd left, we came out from our hiding spot.

"Was that Mrs. Vondrak?" asked Connor Billings.

Mrs. Vondrak was the town librarian. She also played piano at the Methodist church.

Jacob nodded. "She's in on it. She was one of the customers in the grocery store that day."

We scratched our heads.

"Who else is in on it?" asked Josephine Reynolds.

"Saul Hawley and Tina Mueller. They were the other two customers in the store that day," Jacob said. Saul Hawley was a farmer and Tina Mueller was a stay-at-home mom. "Let's see. There's Mr. Munger of course, the store owner. Oh, and we had to get Mark Foltz."

"The Chief of Police?" Cain Sanders asked.

"Well yeah," Jacob said. "How else are we going to safely collect the money? You never *actually* meet at the location on the ransom note. That's a *diversion*. You get a crooked cop to make sure all the other cops are staking out the decoy location. Then you meet somewhere else."

"Oooh," we said. Then we nodded. The decoy location seemed key.

It was silent for a moment.

Sally Winters pointed at the blow-up mattress. "Is he moving at all?" she asked.

Jacob stepped in front of her hand, blocking Sally's view. "He's fine. He's just sleeping," Jacob said. Then Jacob's index finger popped up. "Oh yeah." He looked at Ted Gunderson. "Your dad is in on it, too."

"*My* dad?" Ted asked.

Jacob nodded. "Who do you think sold us the junk car?"

Ted's dad sold used cars. Everyone in town said they were junk.

The meetup was arranged for late Monday night at one in the morning.

"It's the time you'd least expect," Jacob explained at lunch earlier that day. "Nothing is ever happening on a Monday night."

"*Monday Night Football*," said Shane Livingston. But we ignored him.

"Where will the cops be?" asked Marissa Schmitz.

"They will be out by the Sioux River: the decoy location," Jacob said. "While we will be right here in town at the cemetery."

The select five of us got to watch the whole thing. We got there early at 12:30 a.m., and for half an hour, we simply sat in darkness. Then the Milburns' Land Rover pulled into the cemetery. They drove up to the middle, where the large cross tombstone stood. They parked in front of it, their headlights trained on the cross so that we could see everything.

Jacob's mom, wearing a grey hazmat suit, emerged from behind the tombstone. She held little Billy's hand. Gary Milburn jumped out of the car, two huge duffel bags draped over each shoulder. He dashed to his son and fell to his knees. He dropped the duffel bags to his side and said, "It's all there."

Jacob's mom let go of Billy's hand and he ran to his father's arms. Gary kissed the top of his son's head over and over. Then he scooped him up, stuffed him in the car, and the Milburns drove off.

That was it. It was completely dark again.

The Milburns appeared on television, once again reunited with little Billy, all smiles. A journalist for *TIME* wrote an article about them. Some New York author wanted to write a book about the whole thing.

Jacob Carbunkle stayed until the end of the school year.

"You don't move right away," he explained. "That just looks suspicious."

We nodded. But we also high-fived because Jacob had become like the cool older kid who knew all the things that we didn't.

Jacob and his parents moved at the beginning of summer. They told everyone they were moving to Omaha, but that's not actually where they were moving.

"Remember the decoy location?" Jacob said. "It's kind of like that."

We had no idea where they moved to. It gave us more pleasure that way, made Jacob and his parents seem slightly deified. On the day they left, we watched the Carbunkles' blue Subaru head south of town, towards Interstate 29.

"They'll probably turn around once they're down the road," said Connor Billings. "Then they'll head in the opposite direction."

Shortly after they left, several townspeople spent surprising sums of money on things we didn't know they could afford. Chief of Police Mark Foltz took his wife on a Nordic cruise. Saul Hawley, the farmer, bought ten more acres of land near the Sioux River. Tina Mueller, the stay-at-home-mom, started a college fund for her three young children. Mrs. Vondrak digitized our town's miniscule library. Mr. Munger, the grocer, started a Health Foods aisle that even included some organic produce. Ted Gunderson's dad bought six legitimate new cars to sell in the hopes of rebranding his image. And Mrs. Douglas, our seventh-grade teacher, bought one of those cars—a new BMW coupe, no less.

Suspiciously, the Milburns themselves built a new house at the edge of town, a four-bedroom country style with a huge, wraparound porch. They paid for it up front in cash.

That summer, we didn't have our driving permits yet. The Billy Milburn kidnapping was the most interesting thing that had happened in our lives. And without it, we were bored, restless, and empty.

So we rode our bikes around town, shouting at whoever would listen that there were townspeople in on the Billy Milburn kidnapping. We did it for fun, just for something absurd to shout while the sun beat down on our sunburned faces.

We even pointed out those who we knew for a fact were in on it. For example, three of us ran into the grocery store and yelled, "Mr. Munger was in on the Billy Milburn kidnapping!" We did the same thing to Mrs. Vondrak in the library.

In both locations, there was a moment of awkward silence after we'd shouted. Then the customers laughed, as did Mr. Munger and Mrs. Vondrak. Then the customers went back to consulting the labels on the fat-free Greek yogurt cartons or thumbing through books on shelves.

We wrote an anonymous letter to the editor of our town's newspaper. It named everyone who we knew was involved, even insinuated that the Milburns themselves were complicit. It was laughed off, and "Everyone was in on it" became a saying around town.

We even got Marissa Schmitz, who was a lifeguard at the community pool, to pry at Billy one day at swimming lessons.

"Every time I asked him about the Carbunkle's basement," Marissa told us later, "little Billy looked at me like he didn't know what I was talking about. He said, 'Who are the Carbunkles?'"

The next year at Josephine Reynolds' fourteenth birthday party, we remembered fondly how, the year before, Jacob Carbunkle had sat and talked with Tyler the whole night.

"He was vetting him, you know," said Connor Billings.

We were older now. We knew what words like "vetting" meant.

Sally Winters said, "Just think, Josie, if your parents made more money, it would've been Tyler they kidnapped."

Josephine, the birthday girl, chuckled. "You know, you're right," she said. Then she sighed and said, "I could've made some *real* money."

We looked at Tyler. He sat alone on one of the foldout chairs, quietly eating chips and salsa.

He was six now, probably too old by Jacob Carbunkle standards. But he was a very well-behaved boy. Very quiet.

BACKWATER

EVERYONE WAS SHOUTING AND pointing at the muddy river. He went under, they kept saying, he went under. I couldn't move. The foamy white caps danced on the waves, bits of suds torn off and carried away by the wind.

There were ten of us there. The eight who weren't drowning (minus me), dashed across the sandbars, shouting Riley's name over and over. My best friend, Katie, was there. So was the senior boy who liked me. His name was Kevin. The group stopped right at the edge of the last sandbar, right where the actual current started.

I could hear them arguing over whether someone should jump in and try to save Riley. I dug my feet in the sand. I curled my toes forward. I did it so hard it felt like I was crushing the sand into even tinier granules. I was thinking about my dad and seeing his fist slamming on the grand piano keys in our living room. Then I was thinking how Jenna Morehauser, rail-thin in her little yellow bikini, kind of looked like my mom. The affair she had admitted to. At my hips, the phantom touch of Tiago's fingertips. All these things at once.

Then Riley's head popped above the water's surface. He was already some fifty yards downstream. He waved his arms. I snapped out of it and sprinted towards the group at the edge of the sandbar.

When I reached them, Riley disappeared again beneath the current.

It was an accident. Or a coincidence. I don't know which. A few months before the Missouri River pulled Riley under, Katie's orange tabby cat, Ginger, escaped from her house one night. So she drove around our little suburban town of White Lake looking for it. She pulled into the alley behind the yoga studio off Main Street and bam: there in the headlights was my mom and Tiago, lip-locked and holding each other like the couples at our high school in between classes. Blinded by the headlights, they rushed into the studio through the backdoor.

"You're positive it was my mom?" I asked Katie.

We were in my basement bedroom. Right after she'd seen it, she'd driven over.

Katie nodded. "Positive."

"Because it's dark out," I said. "And you said you only saw them for like a second."

"But I saw her hair," Katie said.

My mom had the most distinctive curly red hair.

The only thing we knew about Pranamaya Kosha, the yoga studio, were the rumors that the Portuguese instructor, Tiago, was a bit too handsy with some of the women yogis. Katie and I thought yoga was a goofy thing people did to feel worldly, like drinking herbal tea. But yoga had swept our high school by storm. All the popular skinny girls, like Jenna Morehauser, wore yoga pants to school and had memberships to Pranamaya Kosha, which was another reason we thought it was stupid.

My gut told me Katie was wrong about what she'd seen. For one, eyewitness accounts were notoriously unreliable. I'd seen enough *Law & Order, CSI, NCIS,* and *Law & Order: SVU* to know that. So had Katie. And then there was the simple principle of otherness—meaning sure, people's parents cheated, but *other* people's parents, not mine.

My parents' fighting got worse that spring. It was always about something small that turned into something big. One night after supper, I came up from my basement bedroom to get an ice cream sandwich from the fridge. I could hear them upstairs, arguing over what color to repaint the base trim in the bathroom.

"Blue is a depressing color," my dad said.

"*Dark* blue is depressing. I'll give you that," my mom said. "But not cerulean."

"I don't want to be depressed while I'm brushing my teeth."

"Then don't use the bathroom. Use Ali's bathroom downstairs."

I froze for a second, gripping the handle of the freezer.

Thankfully, my dad shifted gears, alluding to the fact that my mom had been between jobs for a year and a half.

"Okay then. Have fun buying your cerulean paint with your zero income," dad said.

"We have plenty of money," mom countered.

I didn't know if that was true or not, but then again, we did live in White Lake.

Another night, my parents got into it at the supper table over the barbecue sauce on the meatloaf. After his first bite, my dad clanked his fork loudly on his plate.

"This is too damn spicy," he said. He glared at my mom. "What kind of barbecue sauce did you use?"

My mom shrugged. She'd just joined the yoga studio. At least at first, I think she did it for the clothes, because she was so slender and had such long legs and looked good in her tank tops and yoga pants.

My dad got up from the table and walked to the fridge. He threw open the door, pointed inside, and said, "I knew it! You got sweet and *spicy*. I said to get sweet and *tangy*." Then he slammed the door shut.

Physically, he was an unflattering counterpoint to my mom, with short arms and a big belly. His main talent was playing the piano. He played for the Lutheran church we attended.

"I don't have to listen to this," mom said. She glanced at the clock on the microwave. She pulled her curly red hair back into a ponytail, then stood. "I'm going to the seven o'clock at Pranamaya Kosha."

"Where?" dad said.

"The yoga studio," mom said, pushing past him. She slammed the kitchen door on her way out, which was more dramatic than dad's slamming of the refrigerator door because it was so much louder.

Dad marched into the living room and started practicing that Sunday's material.

I strongly suspected that my mom intentionally made that meatloaf with spicy barbecue sauce. She was orchestrating fights, creating excuses to storm out.

No one knew what to do. What do we do, they kept repeating, what do we do? Kevin, the boy who liked me, gripped the sides of his shaggy hair. Riley was one of his best friends. Katie shuffled her feet in panic, her hands clasped at her chest.

Calling 911 seemed like the best idea. Kevin dashed back to the biggest sandbar, about twenty yards from us, the one where all our T-shirts and jean shorts and towels lay strewn about. He dug around for his phone.

"At the old boat docks!" Kevin said. I remember he shouted it into the phone. "We're at the old boat docks!"

"Look!" Jenna Morehauser screamed.

We saw it, too: a dot on the surface of the water 150 yards downstream. It was like a tiny star in the sky. Just for a second. Then it was gone.

To use terminology from my probability and statistics class, there was a direct correlation between the intensity of my parents' fighting and dad's being a psycho at the piano. The church music wasn't that difficult, plus he basically had most of it memorized, so he only practiced for about an hour a couple nights a week. But once the fighting escalated, he started practicing every night. Right after supper, he'd slip silently into the living room and sit down at the grand piano and stay there for hours.

He tried playing more difficult pieces, like Lizst's "Sonata in B minor" or Brahms' "Kavierstucke." But there's a big difference between a suburban WASP church pianist and an actual concert pianist. He sounded like a third-grader clunking the keys for the first time. He'd stop and cuss loudly at his inability to get even a few bars into a piece without screwing up.

One night mom announced at supper she wasn't going to church that Sunday.

Dad clanked his fork. "What? Why not?"

Mom wore a tank top that said "There's No Place Like Om."

"I'm going to the Sunday morning practice at Pranamaya Kosha."

Dad was silent. He breathed loudly through his nostrils. It sounded like he was emitting steam.

I said, "That's the yoga—"

"I know what it is," dad hissed.

I sat up in my chair. Dad's breathing kept getting louder and more forceful. I glanced at mom. She was stiff and wide-eyed. I could tell she was scared, too.

Dad shot up and backwards, the legs of his chair screeching against the wood floor. He held mom's gaze for several seconds. His nostrils flared with each heavy breath. I thought he'd either hit her or break something. It seemed like the inevitable conclusion to such drastic nasal breathing.

Instead, he disappeared into the living room. We heard the piano bench being pulled out, the key cover opening, and sheet music being shuffled into place. Then he flubbed the opening bars of Rachmaninoff's "Prelude in G minor" several times.

Over the sounds of the piano, mom said, "I'm going to the seven." She pointed at the table. "Do you mind cleaning this up?"

She left. Dad played on choppily for a little while. I was taking
his plate of pork chops and mashed potatoes to the sink when he
bashed the keys. I nearly dropped the plate. The first time he did
it, he held his fists down, so the discordant vibrations stayed in the
air, fading out like a departing siren. Then he slammed the keys
again and again.

That scared the shit out of me. It sounded like the piano was a
living organism wailing at dad to let it go free. I couldn't stand to
be there, so I left the kitchen a mess and went to Katie's.

That was exactly one week before Ginger escaped and Katie
would come running over with the news that she'd seen my mom
and Tiago necking behind the yoga studio.

After Katie told me what she'd seen, I observed my mom closely
for signs of adultery. I watched, in the mornings, as she scooped
oatmeal into a bowl. I watched her fill it with water from the sink
and put it in the microwave. I watched her mix in a squirt of sugar
free syrup.

She did this every morning, and from it, I could tell nothing.

I watched her sip coffee at the kitchen table. Her eyes moved
back and forth from the newspaper to *Good Morning America* on the
little TV we had in the kitchen. Dad was already at work. It was
just her and me.

I munched my Lucky Charms and stared, seeing nothing
different but perceiving her as some horribly changed being, a kind
of overgrown monster taking up all the space in the kitchen.

She'd ask something innocuous or school-related. I'd answer
automatically in short clips. I'd think, cleverly: you have no idea
that I know. But I was still somewhat encumbered by doubt or
denial, I don't know which. I'd think: Maybe she's not. Maybe
they're just good friends.

I wanted it to be easier, meaning I wanted her eyes to confess.
I wanted the expression on her bony face to betray guilt. I wanted

her to put down the paper and say, "Ali, there's something I need to tell you." I practically begged her in my mind to open up to me.

But of course she just pointed at Robin Roberts and said, "I'm never cutting my hair that short. Not until I'm like at least seventy."

It was twenty minutes before the ambulance showed up. We met the EMT's at the shore. We had all put our clothes back on by that point, which made the afternoon sun feel hotter. Kevin was freaking out, jumping and pointing at the river behind us. Katie and I were standing next to each other. Katie was crying. She and I didn't know Riley, only knew who he was. This was a group of seniors, and we were freshmen, granted admittance because two boys happened to like us.

I remember thinking, right after it happened, how weird it was that we'd watched it: Riley drowning. Of all the things to see.

I thought about Riley's parents. About them receiving the news. We're sorry, but the Missouri River swallowed your son.

Two state troopers showed up fifteen minutes later with a boat. It took them another five minutes to get it in the water. They warned us not to get our hopes up, then sped off in the direction we pointed.

Once they'd gone, Kevin came over and threw his arms around me. His body was moist with sweat, his shoulders broad.

I didn't go there so much as I found myself there. Dad was at the church for a choir rehearsal and mom had two girlfriends over. They had already drunk one bottle of wine at the kitchen table and were halfway through another.

It was a short walk from our house. It was like I just disap-peared and then reappeared, like the snap of fingers: five minutes before the seven o'clock and I rented a mat, slipped quietly into the studio. Inside, the walls and floor were oak. The room was nearly full, mostly women. They had on tank tops and yoga pants. I had on a T-shirt and gym shorts. I wasn't prepared for how hot it was, like ninety-five degrees. The only spots left were in the back, and I set my mat up in a corner the way the others had.

Tiago emerged from behind a wall at the front. He had long hair pulled back in a ponytail. He was tall and lean and wore a gray tank top that exposed the ropy muscles on his arms and shoulders. He wore matching little gray shorts. The only time I'd seen man shorts that short was on the basketball players in my dad's high school yearbook.

He said something in greeting, but I didn't know what it was. It didn't sound like English. I watched him run his eyes over the women. I imagined that his eyeballs had little magical fingers that reached out and grazed their shoulders and the backs of their necks. He said get into downward dog. I mimicked the woman to my left as best I could.

Tiago meandered leisurely up and down the rows of women, examining butts in the air, hips cocked to the side, thighs straining to maintain balance. Occasionally, he'd place his hands on someone's hips or shoulders or wherever, really. He had free reign, it seemed.

The heat was already getting to me. I was sweating bullets out my forehead, pits, and crotch. A sick feeling welled in my gut. I met eyes with Tiago. He came toward me. I was in warrior one.

He smiled. A small smile, just at one corner of his lips. Then he was in my space, right behind me, his feet on my mat. I held my arms above my head, hands clasped. My legs were on fire, my knees wobbling from the strain.

He cupped his hands over my hips.

I opened my mouth, but nothing came out. Sweat dripped into my right eye. It stung, but it was nothing compared to how bad my legs burned.

"A little lower," Tiago said into my ear.

And I bent my knees further, sunk in deeper.

"Lower."

His fingers hooked onto the bones of my pelvis.

"There."

I closed my eyes, the saltiness prickling under my lids. I thought: why did I come here? What is this place? I'm not sure how long Tiago's hands stayed clamped to me. It was as if I left my body momentarily. Evaporated, perhaps. I lost sensation in the darkness.

When I opened my eyes, Tiago was back up front. He told us to stand straight up.

I slipped out.

Lightheaded, I sucked in the cool, conditioned air of the entryway. A few times, blackness flashed before my eyes. I thought I'd faint.

I drank water from a cooler. A dozen big swallows from the same cone-shaped paper cup, filled over and over. I crumpled it in my hand, then threw it away. I was convinced.

I wiped my brow. Then I walked home, determined.

The river spat Riley out about seven miles downstream from us, on the Nebraska side. The troopers found him on the shore, purple-faced and bloated. They got there just in time. He coughed up buckets of brown water. He was scared out of his mind, but other than that, he was fine.

Of course everyone in White Lake knew about it immediately. They shook their heads at what a foolish showoff Riley had been for trying to swim in the current. Everyone knew you were supposed to stay in the shallow backwaters along the sandbars. A week later at graduation, when Riley crossed the stage to receive his diploma and shake Principal Livingston's hand, it was like watching an ignorant ghost stroll about, unaware that it was supposed to be dead.

My parents weren't at the graduation ceremony. Dad was staying in a motel. He insisted on it, couldn't stand to be in the house. So it was just mom and I. I stayed in the basement, avoided her at all costs. Kevin picked me up for school in the mornings. At night, I got in his car and went wherever he took me: to the Dairy Queen, up and down Main Street, sometimes back to his house.

Katie and I sat in the bleachers, watched our senior boyfriends get their diplomas. Afterwards, in the congratulations line, I kissed Kevin. He'd already been drinking. I could smell it on his breath.

Everyone wanted to shake Riley's hand, as if to feel for themselves he was real. I remember people pointing at Riley's parents and saying, at a respectfully low volume, how lucky they were. How easily the river, if it had wanted, could've taken their son.

How they'd never have gotten over it.

I walked straight home from the studio and asked my mom, right there in the kitchen. Her friends had left. Dad wasn't home yet. She was tipsy. I was still red-faced and sweaty from the yoga heat.

All she said was, "Yes."

"I'm telling dad!"

"He already knows," mom said.

"What?"

Mom nodded. Her eyes were bloodshot, but that was from the wine. I waited for tears to come. Or remorse or pain to show on her face. But she just nodded matter-of-factly. She took another sip of wine.

"He's known for a while," she said.

I didn't know what to say. It didn't make sense to me, that dad would know and not do anything. That everything between them was already on the table, so to speak.

"Let me tell you something, Ali."

I braced for it. The revelation.

She drained her wine glass, then set it down. "Your dad and I were never right for each other. We shouldn't have gotten married."

"What are you talking about?"

She just nodded. Then she looked at me.

"I don't love him."

She said it with ease, like it didn't cost her a thing.

The night of graduation, there was a big bonfire outside of town, out in a pasture somewhere. I didn't, but everyone else got really drunk. Riley the ghost told his harrowing tale of being pulled under and resurfacing, over and over. People hung on his words as he described how his lungs filled with water, how he practically vomited it up each time he surfaced. I could hardly stand to listen. But with each retelling, I found myself pulled under, my own breath growing short as Riley reached the point in the story where he blacked out and next remembered having his chest pressed by a state trooper. I thought of the heat in the yoga studio.

I saw Katie recede from the light of the fire and into the darkness, led by the hand by her boyfriend. Kevin kept tugging at my arm, saying come on, let's do it. But I didn't feel like it and I wouldn't budge. He was slurring his words. A half hour later he retreated into the darkness, went to sleep in the backseat of his car.

Eventually everyone disappeared. And it was just me, standing alone by the dying bonfire. I kept inching closer and closer, because it kept getting colder and colder.

I'd never been out this late. I wanted to go somewhere. So I fished the keys out of Kevin's jean pocket. He barely stirred. I started the car and took off down the highway towards town, Kevin out cold in the backseat.

The one cop in White Lake had long since gone off duty. I went all over. I drove past the high school, through South View and the newer developments, past the Starlite Inn where my dad was staying, past my own house where my mom was sleeping. I drove fast and took corners too sharply. Kevin snored through it all. It was like I had the town to myself, like I'd snuck into an amusement park after hours. I didn't think of anything, really. I just looked at my dark, sleeping town as I rode waves of excitement.

Finally, just before I drove to Kevin's, I stopped in front of Pranamaya Kosha. I was just going to sit a moment and stare. Then I saw it: a furry little orange ball, right there on the sidewalk in front of the studio, faint in the streetlight. I got out of the car. It looked like Ginger, but it was much skinnier. And a patch of fur was missing on its back.

I took a step forward. My foot scraped against the pavement. The cat arched its back and hissed, then darted down the sidewalk. It disappeared around the corner. I thought about giving chase, but something stopped me, like it had on the sandbar.

It was just me, standing on a deserted sidewalk in front of a closed yoga studio. I glanced to my left, stared at the glass storefront, at the pale and dimmed reflection of myself. The funny thing is, two weeks from this night, someone will smash a brick through the exact spot I'm staring at. Tiago will leave town after too many complaints from too many women. One night, after the divorce, at supper in our two-bedroom apartment in Sioux Falls, I'll ask my dad if he was the one who tossed the brick, and he'll deny it. But his face will flush a little. He'll say he doesn't want to talk about it anymore. At the end of summer, Kevin will dump me, then go off to college.

But here's what I want to remember. That I decided right there: I'm going to start saving for a car. That I felt the rush of summer excitement come over me like a wave: the bonfires, the trips to the river, the sweaty backseats, the fireworks, and that in that moment, like Riley, all that really mattered was that I could touch my face and it was there, that I could see my reflection in the window before me, and that if others looked, they could, too.

ABOUT THE AUTHOR

Ross Wilcox is from Elk Point, South Dakota. Currently, he teaches writing at the University of North Texas. His stories have appeared in numerous literary journals. In addition to writing, Ross is a big supporter of the Dallas Mavericks and, sadly, the Dallas Cowboys. For more information, you can visit him at rosswilcox.com, and you can follow him on Twitter @rossofthewilcox.

7.BOOKS